The Girl In The Back Of The Room

The Girl In The Back Of The Room

A NOVEL

(With bonus short story, "The Letter")

Pamela Kay Hawkins

ISBN: 1929257120
ISBN 13: 9781929257126
Library of Congress Control Number: 2015912116
Pamela Kay Hawkins Publishing, LLC
Broken Arrow, OK
ALR 7.25.15

For my grandmother, Lillian, and my mother, Mary, who gave me life, love, and shared friends, especially Jean and Mary Louise. Together they taught me a great deal about what it means to be a woman. And for my granddaughters—Laurel, Aubrey, Madeline, and Lillian—who give me joy every day.

Life never follows the plans you make.
Sometimes I think life has a life of its own.

Table of Contents

CHAPTER 1

The Box In the Attic

LAURIE BILLINGS CLIMBED THE THIRD flight of stairs to the attic door and stopped. Try as she might, she'd never been able just to turn the knob and walk in—at least, not when she was alone. The huge eye of the attic fan stared at her from the staircase wall. She willed herself to peek through its silent blades into the attic beyond. Laurie half-expected someone to meet her gaze. No one ever did. Dust motes drifted in a shaft of filtered light over an ancient steamer trunk. Racks of plastic-covered clothes hung like ghosts off to the side.

"Laura Margaret Billings," she whispered to herself through clenched teeth, "stop acting like some scared little kid. You're almost *fifteen*, and you can *do* this." Laurie took a deep breath and turned the knob.

The hardwood floor creaked as Laurie crossed the attic threshold. The very air told her she'd stepped into another world: "Definitely *not* Oz or Narnia," she said aloud and immediately wished she hadn't.

The walls sucked up her words like a silent vacuum. She forgot to breathe. Her heart pounded, shaking her as she stood holding onto the doorknob. She fought the urge to run back down the stairs, to find her mother and grandmother. Somewhere, in the lived-in part of the house, they chatted away, oblivious to the secret, spellbound world of the third floor. It did not call to them as it did to her. They did not creep up the stairs and pause before the attic door, afraid to trespass. No, they climbed the stairs and opened the door and got whatever it was they'd come for and walked out again, chattering all the while, as if the third floor were just an attic and all the magic gone. And so they did not mind her going, for they could not see the danger.

Her heart quieted, and she could almost breathe again, though the attic air, thick and heavy, clung to her lungs like a woolen blanket. Summer had given way to autumn elsewhere in the world, but here it lay packed away with all of its heat and none of its brightness. Laurie let go of the doorknob and left the door ajar. The fresh cool air tried to enter, but the attic's heat overpowered it as it rushed past, down the stairs, into the lower regions of the house. Her grandmother's admonitions about utility bills echoed in her mind, but Laurie didn't close the door. Somehow she knew that if she closed the door, it would stick, and she would be shut up here forever, forgotten as easily as the steamer trunk or the outmoded clothes.

"Why do I put myself through this?" Laurie asked.

This time she did not listen to the walls. She did not listen to anything but the sound of her feet clacking loudly across the attic floor, away from the plastic ghosts and the silent steamer. She walked down the deserted hall, trying not to run, and did not let herself glance into the empty rooms as she passed. Instead, she fixed her gaze on the doorway at the end of the corridor, the entrance to the attic sanctuary, her favorite place—better even than the secret passage that ran between the walls. A board creaked behind her in the hall, and she bolted the last few feet into the north bedroom. Safe! Laurie knew better than to look behind her. Whatever followed would not enter here. She would deal with leaving later.

North light flooded the room through quaint dormer windows. Of all the rooms on the third floor, this alone looked as if it were inhabited by the living. A nightstand, complete with lamp and book, rested next to the large double bed. The bed was made, its pillows plump in their lace-trimmed shams. A handmade quilt lay folded at the footboard. A dresser was situated nearby, a silver-trimmed brush and comb set placed neatly on top next to an antique, porcelain washbasin and pitcher. There was a rocking chair with a braided pad in the seat and a floor lamp next to it. A small chest, which Laurie knew was papered inside with tiny blue flowers, snuggled next to the foot of the bed. Large bookcases, crammed with books, stood on either side of the doorway and on either side of the window seat. Laurie knelt on the seat and released the latches and pushed the windows wide. She loved this room that was somehow her with its old books and old windows. How glorious were windows without screens or storm coverings, windows, which opened onto the world and let it come in. She sat on the bench seat and reveled in the crisp autumn air and her irrepressible joy: "*This* is why I come," she said to the ceiling. She jumped up and spread her arms wide and twirled around like a five-year-old, until giddiness forced her to plop down on the flower-patterned rug and wait until the room stopped spinning as well.

As the room slowed to a stop, Laurie spied a box underneath the bed. She crawled over and dragged it out. It was an old cardboard box and very dusty. In her mother's handwriting a label proclaimed: "Meg's Memories."

"How fun!" Laurie said, wondering briefly if she should open it. Nothing was forbidden on the third floor, not even the wonderful costumes from the amateur theatricals when her grandmother was a girl. Once her grandmother had played Josephine March in a neighborhood production of *Little Women*, and the experience made such a lasting impression that she had named her only daughter—Laurie's mother—after the oldest March girl, Margaret, better known to everyone as "Meg." Meg Billings was aptly named, Laurie thought, since she seemed to share more than a few of the March girl's characteristics. Secretly, Laurie wished her mother were more like "Jo," short for Josephine March, the next oldest girl of the four little women. Laurie smiled to herself as she thought about the old costume—Jo's dress—with its hoop skirt that flew up in front whenever Laurie tried to sit down in it. She thought about getting it, putting it on again, and pretending she was Jo, but that meant going back down the hall and into the west room . . . No, she'd open the box. Attic boxes always held surprises.

Laurie removed the top and took the box to the window seat. A dried corsage with three rosebuds lay on top of a bunch of old letters, tied with a ribbon. She carefully removed the corsage and set it on the windowsill, along with the letters, which were obviously private. Next were a jumble of old photographs, torn movie stubs and assorted programs, some folded documents which looked boring, and, wedged in the cardboard at the very bottom, a picture of a young man in a military uniform. Cute.

She recognized most of the people in the photographs: relatives and her mother's friends, much younger and looking silly in the dated clothes of the early 1940s. Laurie found a picture of her mother, sitting under an enormous elm—the same tree that grew up beside her window seat. She looked out of the window, down through the branches, to the same spot where her mother had sat in the picture. Strange. She stared at the picture: Meg looked about Laurie's age.

Laurie walked to the mirror and held the picture next to her face. The resemblance was almost scary. "Well, what do you know?" Laurie said, surprised that they looked so much alike. They weren't built alike, and their coloring was different, but if she covered up the Forties' pompadour and imagined Meg with a Sixties' hairstyle—a flip, maybe, like her own . . . She looked at the double reflection, until it made her nervous, and she retreated to the window seat.

She tossed the picture into the box and rummaged around until she found another picture of her mother standing beside the cute guy in uniform. She picked up his picture again and turned it over. Written on the back was his name: Lawrence James Lightman. She'd seen the name somewhere before. She glanced at the letters on the windowsill and saw a return address on the top letter: J. Lightman, from Topeka, Kansas.

"Well, Mom," Laurie said, holding up the picture of them together, "just who is this mysterious Mr. Lightman? And does Daddy know about him?" She laughed, thinking how much fun she'd have teasing her mother about the luscious Mr. L. "Definitely material for serious kidding, Mom. Now, let's see what else you've been keeping from me."

Laurie sifted through the rest of the pictures, but found nothing exciting. She saved the folded papers for last, knowing from experience that official-looking papers, usually expired insurance policies, were always the dullest. This time she was wrong.

The first paper was a hospital birth certificate complete with the baby's footprints and the mother's thumbprint, which were about the same size. Laurie stood up and put the paper on the floor. It was hard to believe that anyone started with feet that tiny. She picked up the paper and turned it over to read the other stuff— the boring stuff about location, names, and dates. But it wasn't boring at all: Mother's name—Margaret Alice *Lightman*; Father's name—Lawrence James Lightman; Baby's name—*Laura Margaret Lightman*.

"Something's wrong." Laurie picked up the other paper—a marriage license for Margaret Alice Tidwell and Lawrence James Lightman. This can't be *my* birth certificate, she thought. I'm Laura Margaret *Billings*.

Laurie heard someone coming up the stairs to the attic, heard her mother calling her, heard the footsteps getting closer to her room.

"Laurie, didn't you hear me calling you?" Meg said, smiling in the doorway. "Good heavens, child, what have you found now?"

Laurie looked at her and tried to answer, but no words came. She held out the papers.

CHAPTER 2

What's In a Name?

LAURIE WATCHED AS HER MOTHER crossed the room and took the papers from her hand. Meg's smile evaporated like a drop of water caught by a flame as she looked at them, and Laurie wished with all her heart she'd stayed downstairs today and never ventured into the attic. Hadn't she always known that the attic was a dangerous place, full of ghosts and dead things that reached out, trying to grab her, to hurt her, to drag her back into their world of darkness and death? It had never occurred to her that it could reach for her mother as well.

"Mom? Are you all right?"

"Where did you find these?" Meg nodded at the papers, then dropped them onto the floor. Her voice sounded hollow and accusing. She sat down beside Laurie on the window seat, but her presence did not comfort.

"They were in this box." Laurie picked up the open box and handed it to her mother.

Meg took it and glanced at the contents, then picked up the picture of the man in the uniform. She looked at him for a moment, then put the picture back: "It used to have a lid. Where's the lid?"

Laurie got up and retrieved the cardboard top from the floor by the bed. Its label, wiped clean of the dust on the rest of the box top, seemed to yell at her: "Meg's Memories." Her fingerprints were everywhere. Avoiding her mother's eyes, Laurie handed the lid to her mother: "Careful; it's awfully dusty."

"It hasn't been opened in a very long time." Meg slowly traced the label with her index finger, framing it in the dust. "To tell you the truth," she said, glancing up at Laurie, "I'd forgotten it existed. But . . . here it is again."

They sat in silence for a few moments. Laurie didn't know what to think: her mother seemed suddenly different from the person she'd known all of her life. She looked older, but it was more than that: she *was* another person, a person called Margaret Lightman. And if the birth certificate for Laura Margaret Lightman was hers, well, then, wasn't *she* another person, too—a person with a father named James Lightman, not Eric Billings? Eric Billings had two children named Ruthie and Stevie; he didn't have a daughter named Laurie at all. Did that mean that she had no brother or sister? Or did she have brothers and sisters she didn't even know? Laurie rubbed her eyes: her head ached. A sudden thought crossed her mind: maybe it wasn't her birth certificate— after all, she hadn't checked the birthdate. Maybe Meg had had a baby before—a baby who died—and she'd just named Laurie the same thing. That would explain everything—why her mother seemed so sad, almost angry that Laurie had discovered the box. Her mind raced ahead: Yes, Meg had been married before to this Lightman person. They'd had a baby and the *both* of them, the baby *and* the husband, had been killed, probably in some kind of terrible accident! Then Meg had met Eric Billings, they'd fallen in love, married, and then they'd had her and named her after the poor baby who'd died! It made sense . . .

"Laurie, I'm so sorry." Meg put her arm around Laurie's shoulders and drew her close. Her voice shook with emotion. "I should have told you about this a long time ago."

"No, Mama. It's OK." Laurie pulled away so she could see her mother's face. "*I'm* sorry I got into your things and made you remember. It must have been so awful! I can't imagine what you must've gone through!"

Meg looked out the window at something Laurie couldn't see: "At the time I thought I wouldn't live through it." She turned to Laurie and smiled. "I was so young when it all happened. When you're young things have a way of looking much worse than they really are. Actually, when I look back on it, I'm glad it happened—"

"Glad?" Laurie was shocked. "How could you possibly be glad?"

"Well," Meg sighed, "for one thing, I have you, and I have Eric." Meg patted Laurie's knee. "I won't say what I went through was easy—it was one of the hardest things in my life—but, believe me, I'm much happier with Eric than I ever was or ever could be with Jim Lightman."

"But what about the baby?" Laurie felt confused, and there was an uncomfortable lump forming in her throat.

"Laurie, what are you talking about? What baby?"

"The one on the birth certificate, the one that died—"

"Died?" Meg sat up very straight and stared into Laurie's eyes. Then she hugged her: "Oh, baby, is that what you thought? Honey, nobody died; that baby is *you*. Didn't you read the name on the certificate?" Meg smoothed Laurie's hair with her hand. "I thought you understood—"

Laurie struggled to free herself from her mother's arms. She was suddenly angry.

"Understand? Why *would* I understand? Understand what? That I'm somebody else, somebody named Laura *Lightman*? How would I understand that? That some guy that I've never seen or heard of before is my father? I'm supposed to understand that, too, I suppose! Pardon me if I'm stupid, but I guess I just don't understand why you've been lying to me all of these years about something so unimportant as who I really am, 'cause it's for sure I'm not really Laurie *Billings*!"

Laurie jumped up and ran past her mother, out of the room, down the attic hall, and down the three flights of stairs to the ground floor. Out of the corner of her eye, Laurie saw her grandmother in the sunroom—"Laurie! For heaven's sake, child"—but she didn't stop or hear the rest; the screen door slammed behind her, as she bolted out of the house toward the large pine tree in the backyard, where they couldn't get to her, even if they knew where she was, and started to climb.

Laurie sat in her favorite perch near the top of the tree in a platform formed by the conjunction of three large branches. Through the years the bark had worn away, and the resulting effect rather reminded her of a sixteenth century Italian chair she'd seen in one of her mother's interior decorating books. On ordinary days, she would bring her charcoal and sketchpad, or a book, and sketch or read in her tree-chair. Sometimes she just came to think or to listen to the sound of the wind. She loved it up here—loved looking down on the world, loved the gentle swaying of the tree around her, loved the Christmas smell of pine which permeated her senses and drove out all thought of the merely ordinary. But today was not ordinary; today pine mingled with the pungent scent of cedar and stung her nose and made her eyes water.

Laura saw her grandmother and mother searching for her in the yard below. She heard their voices calling her, her name floating up in little gasps, but she did not answer, and she knew they could not see her, even if they knew where she was. The wind came in surprising gusts and handled the needle clusters around her like a fan dancer wielding fans, tantalizing while concealing. She listened intently, trying to understand the bits and pieces of conversation that flew by her on the air. She heard the tremble in her mother's voice, heard the clear, comforting treble of her grandmother's replies, but could not understand the words. For a moment she thought it might be better if she climbed down and pretended that she hadn't known they were looking for her and that everything was all right again. But it wasn't all right, and there had been enough pretending, so she leaned back against the familiar tree trunk and tried not to hear their voices.

After a while Laurie saw them go into the breezeway between the house and the garage apartment where the servants used to live when her mother was growing up and very young. They sat and talked there for a while; Laurie could see them through the branches.

It was nearly sunset when Laurie saw her mother's car pull out of the driveway and head toward their home. She watched, incredulous, as the car turned right, down a side street, and disappeared from her view.

"Laurie?" Her grandmother's voice came from far below the branch.

Laurie saw her looking straight up, trying to see where Laurie sat, but Laurie knew she couldn't really see her through the tangle of needles and branches.

"Laurie, your mother has gone home. Don't you think it's time you came down out of that tree and started acting your age?"

Laurie sat still and said nothing.

"Fine. Suit yourself, but the sun's going down, and it will be getting pretty chilly before long. If you decide to join the human race, I'll be in the house where it's warm, fixing dinner." Her grandmother turned away and started walking toward the house.

"Nana?" Laurie tried not to sound desperate, but was relieved to see her grandmother turn back toward her tree.

"Yes?"

"I'll be right down."

"I'm pleased to hear it. I'll meet you inside."

CHAPTER 3

Ordinary Things

⟳

"SET THE TABLE IN THE sunroom for me," Nana said, as Laurie came into the kitchen. She stood by the stove, her back to Laurie, and she spoke without turning around, so Laurie couldn't tell anything about her mood from looking at her face. "Use the white, woven placemats in the third drawer down, please," Nana continued in a tone of voice that communicated nothing.

"What are we having?" Laurie asked in the same even tone, as she paused in front of the silverware drawer.

"Well, I hadn't counted on company for dinner, so we're just having soup and sandwiches. It's Harriet's night off, you know."

"Are you sure you want me to stay and eat with you tonight?" Laurie asked.

Nana turned around and faced her. She did not smile, but her expression was not angry. Laurie stopped holding her breath and waited for an answer.

"Laurie, I'm not going to lie to you and tell you I'm overjoyed that you're staying with me tonight—"

"Staying with you? But—"

"Please do not interrupt me while I'm speaking."

"I'm sorry, Nana. I won't do it again."

"I should hope not. Go ahead and get the soupspoons and knives—you'd better get salad forks as well. I think I'll make a salad for us, too." Nana turned back to the stove and continued talking. "Harriet made some of her clam chowder Friday, so I'd have something to heat up tonight. There's plenty for both of us. I swear that woman makes the best soups in the world. Have you ever had Harriet's clam chowder?"

"I think so."

Laurie knew so. Harriet had cooked her Manhattan-style clam chowder for them the last time she'd spent the night with her grandmother, before her grandfather had died. The only kind of clam chowder Laurie liked was the white, New England style, but Papa had loved the red Manhattan, so Harriet made it frequently. Laurie didn't think tonight was the right time to complain about the soup. She opened the silverware drawer, got out the utensils, and walked over to the drawer where the placemats were kept.

"Best stuff I ever put in my mouth," Nana continued. "She knows I like certain things, and she spoils me almost as much as she did Alan when he was alive." Nana paused to taste the soup. "Um, um . . . it's almost ready." She put down the spoon and opened the broiler section of the ancient gas range that every woman in the family coveted. "The sandwiches are just about done, too. You'd better get that table set. Dinner will be ready in about five minutes."

"I'll be right back," Laurie said.

Laurie walked out of the kitchen, through the darkened formal dining room, into the brightly lit sunroom. The sun had set, but Nana had turned on the table lamps and everything was bathed in soft, golden light. Laurie loved this room, which was small in comparison to most rooms in the house and cozy. All of Nana's furniture was beautiful—the woods polished to a flawless sheen, the upholstery elegant, the leather soft and luxurious, the colors impeccable—but in the sunroom, the furniture seemed to beckon, to ask her to sit down and relax. Even the sea-green of the grass paper on the walls soothed and comforted like a cool washcloth on a fevered forehead.

Laurie cleared off the table and set it to comply with her grandmother's strict standards of propriety and etiquette. In her whole life, Laurie had never seen her grandmother allow a ketchup bottle or any other original container of foods on the table. Butter was served in a sterling silver butter dish; salt and pepper in silver shakers; condiments, such as ketchup and mustard, in their own small bowls, complete with serving spoons; sauces and salad dressings in cut-glass cruets. It was a major pain to go to all that trouble every time she set her grandmother's table, Laurie thought, but it was also kind of fun, sort of like dressing up in costume, or stepping out of the twentieth century to live for awhile in the nineteenth. Nana was, Laurie decided, not so much a relic of the past, as she was a perfect product of her time and upbringing. Sometimes Laurie even wished that everyone required the same adherence to decorum as her grandparents always had. Rules, painted in black and white and never in shades of gray, were comforting in a way: she always knew where she stood and exactly what was expected of her. *I wonder what Papa and Nana thought about Mom's marriage to Jim Lightman? I wonder what they thought when it ended?*

"Laurie, would you get the tray for me? It's too heavy for me to carry," Nana said, as she carefully negotiated the one step down into the sunroom. "Oh, and child?"

"Yes?" Laurie was already halfway across the dining room.

"Help yourself to something to drink. I didn't know what you'd want."

"I'll be right back with the tray," Laurie said, but stopped as she watched her grandmother try to pull out her chair. "Do you need some help?"

"Thank you, no, Laurie," Nana replied in a silvery, amused voice. "I really can manage; it just takes me longer than it used to."

Laurie saw her smile, and she was suddenly glad for the unexpected turn of events that left her here alone with Nana.

The tray—hand-painted, gilt-edged—held a meal so expertly arranged that Laurie thought it worthy of some fancy restaurant, even down to a tiny, silver vase with a single white chrysanthemum. To Laurie's delight, the flower complemented the small tureen of creamy, white, *New England* clam chowder. Two sliced tomato and cucumber salads, carefully arranged in an alternating pattern, sat beside two large dinner plates each of which held a soup bowl surrounded by delicate, golden fingers cut from grilled cheese sandwiches. The tray was heavy, but she managed to transport it to the sunroom, unload it, and take the empty tray back without spilling a drop or doing anything improperly.

The meal passed in amiable silence much to Laurie's surprise. She had expected some sort of scolding, if not for upsetting her mother (she was sure no one was concerned about *her* discomfort: adults had a tendency to stick together), then certainly for sitting up in the tree, ignoring the summons from below. It occurred to her that the simple dinner preparations, the return to familiar routine, helped somehow to make the revelation of the day dwindle in size, if not in importance. By dessert it resembled a boulder she thought she could scale, if not with ease, then at least with proper climbing gear. The problem was how best to approach it . . .

"We'll leave the dishes for Harriet," Nana said, folding her napkin and moving from the table to her favorite easy chair. "Just take them back into the kitchen and leave them on the counter. It's time we had a talk."

CHAPTER 4

The Box Theory

A KNOT FORMED IN LAURIE'S stomach and grew tighter as she cleared the table.

I knew it was too good to last, Laurie thought, as she sat down across from her grandmother and waited.

Five minutes passed before Nana said a word, time in which Nana gathered her glasses, current needlepoint project, and adjusted the light to suit her.

"Your mother tells me you're upset about Jim Lightman," Nana said, briefly looking over the top of her glasses at Laurie before rummaging in her sewing bag for something.

"How could I be upset about him? I don't even know him," Laurie said.

"Don't take that tone of voice with me, Miss," Nana pulled a skein of sky blue yarn out of her supplies and threaded her needle with a doubled strand. "I'm your grandmother, not your enemy."

She turned the canvas over, revealing a basket weave pattern as neat as the front design, and drew the ends of the thread through until they were hidden, turned the piece over, and began to sew. She seemed quite relaxed, as if there were nothing at all upsetting about the topic currently under discussion.

"I know. I'm sorry." Laurie paused to gather her thoughts. "It's just that Mom and Dad—he *is* still my dad, isn't he?"

Nana nodded and continued sewing.

"Well, they've been lying to me all these years, not just about Mom's not being married before, but about who I *am*. If I hadn't seen that stuff in the attic today, I never would have known that Jim Lightman—my own *father*—even existed. It's not a little white lie to me; it's a big, fat, ugly, black one. Don't you see?"

"Technically, they never lied to you at all—"

"How can you *say* that?"

"Well, legally, you are Laurie Billings and Eric Billings's daughter—Eric adopted you shortly after Meg and he married. You were just about a year old, and he adored you. As far as Eric's concerned, he *is* your real father—much more of a father, I might add, than Jim Lightman would *ever* have been. And did they ever say that your mother hadn't been married before?" Nana looked over the rims of her glasses at Laurie.

"Of course not. The subject never came up."

"Exactly." Nana resumed her needlepoint.

"But that doesn't change the fact that Billings is not the name I was born with, and they knew it and didn't tell me."

"Laurie, would it really have made any difference? You'd still be Laurie Billings now, and you've been Laurie Billings for fourteen, almost fifteen years." Nana stopped sewing and let her work rest in her lap. "Names are really not that important, you know. My last name wasn't always Tidwell—"

"That's different, and you know it—"

"I'll thank you not to speak to me in that tone, young lady. I'm still your grandmother, and you're still my granddaughter, regardless of what your last name is or was, and I will *not* tolerate being talked back to. Is that understood?"

Laurie sighed inwardly but didn't let it show: "Yes, ma'am . . . But it *is* different, isn't it? After all, you had a choice when you married Papa and took his name. I didn't."

"Are you telling me you don't like the name Billings or that you don't like having Eric as a father?"

"Billings is OK, I guess, and Daddy's fine . . . It's just that I feel like the rug's been pulled out from under me: suddenly, Daddy's not Daddy anymore, and someone named Lawrence James Lightman—someone I've never met before—is my real father."

"Laurie, let's get one thing straight right now: there's a lot more to being someone's *real* father than simply getting their mother pregnant."

"Nana!"

"It's true, and what's more, you know it."

"But my father never had a chance to do those things with me—"

"Believe me, honey, Jim Lightman didn't want the chance."

"How do you know?

"Because Eric had to have his permission to adopt you after the divorce, and because Jim didn't care enough about his parental rights to show up in court at the adoption hearing. That's how I know—that, and he's never so much as written one word in all of your fourteen years to find out how you were."

It was so quiet in the minutes that followed that Laurie heard each second passing. How could it be that her own father didn't care about her? She was only a baby when he left her. Why didn't he want her? Somehow the information didn't make sense: her stomach ached, and she was suddenly tired.

Nana put her hand on Laurie's shoulder: "Forgive me, sweetheart. I shouldn't say things like that. Frankly, I'm surprised thinking about that man can still make me this angry. It was all so long ago . . ." Her voice trailed off and silence flooded the room again. Nana patted Laurie's shoulder quickly and sat back in her chair.

"There is something I want you to think about though, Laurie. I don't think it came as a surprise to God that Meg married Jim Lightman, nor was it a shock to Him that the marriage only lasted a year. I think He planned it that way."

Laurie looked up at her grandmother. "I thought you always said God hated divorce—"

"Oh, He does," she said, nodding as she pulled the blue yarn through the canvas, and pushed it back through again, "but that doesn't mean He doesn't use it for His purposes on occasion."

"I don't understand. What purpose?"

"Why getting you here, of course." Nana smiled and deftly ran the remaining thread underneath the basket weave on the back. She bent over her sewing basket and pulled out a long piece of sage green yarn, doubled it, and rethreaded her embroidery needle.

"I think I'll work on the tree for awhile," she said, holding up the canvas for Laurie to see. "Pretty, isn't it?"

Laurie nodded.

Nana attached the thread to the back and resumed her work. "Sometimes, I embroider, and I start thinking how marvelous and strange and wonderfully complicated life is. See this?" Nana turned the canvas so that its back faced Laurie. "It doesn't seem to have anything at all to do with the picture on the front, does it?"

"No," Laurie answered and quietly wondered what it had to do with anything at all. To be polite she added: "I always wondered how you could get the back to look like that, though. Mine always looks like a mess with knots and ends of thread everywhere."

"Mine used to look like yours, too. I just learned a new technique—I'll show you how to do it sometime, if you'd like—"

"Is it hard?"

Nana smiled: "No, it's not hard at all; you just have to follow a pattern when you stitch, instead of just going any which way you please." She looked at the back of her work again and smiled. "I used to think there wasn't any pattern in my life, or anyone else's for that matter, especially when things weren't going the way I thought they should. Life looked like the back of one of your pieces of needlepoint—neither rhyme nor reason to any of it, and ugly. Parts of life are ugly when all you can see are the parts. I felt like that when Meg ran off and married Jim Lightman."

"Mom ran off?"

"Practically. She knew your grandfather and I couldn't stand him, although I'll tell you now that we really had no good reasons for not liking the boy, then—"

"Then why didn't you like him?"

Nana frowned and rubbed her forehead, as if her head hurt. "There was just something about him I didn't trust, and Alan didn't like him, either, said he was a donkey disguised as a thoroughbred"—she laughed as she said it—"He was, too—disguised, I mean—and smooth as melted chocolate with your mother. He was good-looking—"

"I saw his picture."

"Did you?" Nana peered over the rim of her glasses and nodded. "Well, then, you know where your looks come from. You've got Meg's eyes and her nose, but everything else is pure Lightman."

"Do I really look like him?" Laurie wasn't sure she knew how she felt about looking like someone she didn't know.

"Oh, yes." Nana stopped, as if she were going to say more, then bent over and rummaged through her sewing basket, finally finding a small, magnifying glass. She reached up and adjusted the lampshade of her lamp, so that more light shone on the needlepoint. She positioned the magnifying glass over a portion of her work, then stopped, anchoring her needle in the canvas.

"I think I'll put this up until tomorrow. My eyes aren't what they used to be."

"Nana?"

"Yes?"

"Why didn't they stay together?"

"Because God wanted you to have Eric Billings as a father."

"No, seriously."

"I *am* serious." Nana placed her needlepoint in the basket and sat forward in her chair. "Remember the back of your needlepoint?"

Laurie nodded.

"Well, to us then, and to you now, the whole situation looked like that mess. Your mother found out she was pregnant with you the month after their honeymoon. Having a baby the first year of his marriage was not in Jim Lightman's master plan—"

"You mean he didn't want me?"

"It wasn't that he didn't want *you*, he just didn't want the responsibility of being anyone's father. He didn't want any baby in his life then, and he made that quite clear to your mother. He made her life miserable after that; finally, she had no choice but to divorce him."

"I don't understand—"

"You'll have to find out the details from your mother. It's not my place to tell you. But I will tell you that your father got mumps shortly after the honeymoon—"

"Mumps?"

"Mumps. After that, Jim Lightman couldn't father any more children. You're his only offspring."

"So you're saying God made my father sterile?" Laurie was incredulous.

"No, I'm saying God made sure you were conceived before your father got mumps. It's a matter of timing—one month later and there would have been no Laurie Lightman to become Laurie Billings. I think God really wanted *you* here, and, let's face it, without Jim Lightman, you wouldn't be.

"Think about it a moment, Laurie. Think about all the people, over all the intervening years, who had to come together at just the right time for there to be a Laurie Billings. If I hadn't married your grandfather, for instance, I wouldn't have had your mother, and you wouldn't be here—some other little girl, perhaps, but not you."

"So you think God cares whether or not I was born instead of that other little girl?" Laurie shook her head. "I can't see that He's so involved." Laurie looked at her grandmother. "If He is . . . well, what about kids who are born to parents that abuse them, or who starve to death in some foreign country because of a famine or something? Is God responsible for them, too? Is that what He had in mind for them?" Laurie folded her arms and stared at her grandmother.

Nana smiled softly: "Laurie, I'm no theologian, but I do know the Bible says that God is involved with each child even in the womb, and that children are a reward, and that the number of days allotted to each person is written down—set—even before they have lived one. So, yes, I believe God is intimately involved in each person's life." Nana sat back in her chair. "I have a theory about why some children have such a hard time in life, while others don't. Want to hear it?"

"Sure." Laurie did want to hear how Nana could explain God's involvement in all the pain and suffering children went through. Secretly, she didn't think Nana could, or anyone else for that matter.

"It's my 'Box Theory.' See, I think God's reasons for being born are much different from what people think they should be.

If you or I were in charge, we'd think the best possible thing for everyone would be to be born into the best possible circumstances. Right?"

Laurie nodded, and sat back in her chair.

"And we think that means healthy, perfectly formed, with enough food to eat all of the time, and, probably we'd want their parents to be wonderful people, who were caring and probably rich, just so that their children could have every advantage money could buy." Nana stopped and smiled.

"Well, of course," Laurie said, a bit defensively. "Who wouldn't want that for their children?"

"Sometimes I think God doesn't want that—not because He doesn't want children to be happy and healthy, but because He knows what each one of us needs to accomplish His purpose in our lives."

"Which is what? To make us work really hard for what we get, or just to make us miserable?" Laurie was getting tired of this.

"Neither. God puts us here to know Him, so that this life isn't all we have of what He wants us to experience. For some people, having it easy all of their lives is just fine and is never a hindrance to their spiritual well-being. But for others, like me for instance"—Nana laughed—"who are too darned stubborn to think they need anyone other than themselves in this life, God knows a few well-chosen obstacles will help them more than any so-called blessings ever will. So He puts every single person ever born in a box—the box is what you are given, that you haven't any say in, like what sex you are, what country you're born in, what your financial situation is growing up, what situations come your way . . ." Nana's voice trailed off for a moment.

Laurie was grateful for the respite: something about Nana's theory was beginning to make sense.

"You can probably come up with a lot more," Nana continued, "like the circumstances surrounding your conception, but the important point is that you have no control over any of these things: they're just given to you. What you *do* have control over is how you respond to those 'gifts'. And how you respond, my dear, will bring you closer to God, or drive you farther from Him. The important thing to remember is that God has given each person the best 'box' for that particular individual, and that God's purpose is always—*always*—in the best interest of that person, whatever you and I may think his or her circumstances *look like* on the surface."

It was obvious to Laurie that the theological lecture was over, and that Nana felt her point had been made. Laurie wasn't at all sure she bought it.

"So, you're telling me God engineered my circumstance for my ultimate good, that He wanted me to be born, but he didn't want Jim Lightman to act as my father? I'm sorry, Nana, but I'm not so sure this 'gift,' as you call it, is better for me than having my mother and real father stay married. I think you just don't like Jim Lightman, because he did something that hurt your daughter."

"Oh, honey, that's true: I don't like Jim Lightman, because he hurt my Meg. But don't think I'm basing my 'Box Theory' on this one situation. I may not be right about it, but up till now it's made more sense than anything else I've heard. And you don't have to believe me, Laurie. It's just something I wanted to share with you, and maybe give you something to think about." Nana stood up.

"I don't know about you, but I'm getting sleepy. I made up the bed for you in your mother's old room. You know where the towels and everything are."

Nana hugged Laurie and kissed her on the cheek. "Good night, sweetheart. Thank you for listening to my lecture. I don't know, you may be right, but I'm awfully glad you're my granddaughter, and you'll let an old lady think you're here by divine decree and not just an accident, won't you?"

Laurie laughed and hugged Nana back. "Oh, I suppose so, if it's really that important to you."

"If you need anything, just let me know."

"I will, Nana. Good night."

"Good night, honey. Sweet dreams."

CHAPTER 5

The Thing About Boys

THE TWIG CLICKED ACROSS THE slats of the picket fence, reminding Laurie of the train she had heard passing through town last night, as she lay in her bed unable to sleep. The rhythm pulsed through the twig, into her hand, up her arm, and into her head, until she thought the twig dragged her instead of the other way around. Laurie stopped suddenly and threw the twig onto the sidewalk, as if it were a bug she'd found crawling on her hand. She waited for a moment, half expecting it to move, then glanced down the street. No one had seen. She took a deep breath of the crisp autumn air and thought of apples.

Apples. Laurie never thought of apples until fall. Only then were apples dependable, trustworthy. At other times of the year, they looked the same, but she never knew, could never be sure. They could feel like autumn apples—hard, firm to the touch—but touch and sight alone could be deceiving. True apples crunched deliciously when she ate them; pseudo-apples, disguised in apple apparel, yielded only apple-flavored mush, which she immediately spat out. One bite was enough to know which was which. She disliked deceit of any kind. But with false apples, her dislike turned to hatred. Apples were supposed to be food she could count on for her well-being: *An apple a day/ keeps the doctor away.* Apples were supposed to be apples all of the time, but they weren't. They were only really apples in their season.

She began walking again without noticing, her feet traveling automatically toward school, as if her mind resided in her loafers. She felt disembodied this morning, disoriented in a way that could not be attributed to her usual tendency to daydream.

Today, she thought, *I am someone else, someone I don't know.*

"Hey, Laurie, wait up!"

Laurie turned toward the sound, surprised to find herself halfway up the school steps, and saw Jack Dawson coming toward her. She smiled and waited for him to catch up.

"Where were you, anyway?" Jack said, as he reached her step.

"What do you mean?"

"I mean I've been trying to get your attention for the last two minutes. What's up?"

"Sorry. I was just thinking—"

"About what?" Jack pushed open the door and held it while Laurie went in.

"Thanks," Laurie said, thinking Jack was probably the only boy in the world who would bother to open doors for her. It was one of the reasons she liked him. Somehow Jack always made her feel special. "Want to come with me? I left my books in my locker."

"Sure, why not?"

They walked down the west hallway past look-alike gray metal lockers to Laurie's, distinguishable from the others only by its number and bright blue combination lock.

"So what's the big deal?" Jack asked, as Laurie spun the dial to the right.

"Huh?"

"The thing you were thinking so hard about—"

"Oh, that." Laurie grinned up at him, thinking how nice it was to have to look *up* at someone for a change. "It was nothing really; I was just thinking." Laurie turned the dial to the left, then back to the right, and opened her locker.

"Well, if you don't want to tell me, why don't you just say so?"

"OK, I don't want to tell you," she said, reaching into the locker and getting her English Lit. and Algebra I textbooks. She glanced sideways at Jack while she picked up her notebook from the locker floor. He looked so forlorn, that she immediately regretted teasing him. "Hey, I was just kidding!" Laurie flashed a grin, then slammed the locker door and twirled the dial on the lock. "Ready?"

Jack nodded, shifted his books onto his hip, but said nothing.

"Lighten up, will you?" Jack's stony silence bothered her. She sighed deeply. "OK, if you *must* know, I was thinking about apples."

"Apples?"

Laurie nodded: "Now, aren't you sorry you made such a big deal out of it?"

They continued down the hall in easy silence. Just before they reached their homeroom, Jack said: "No joke, apples?"

Laurie raised her eyebrows and grinned: "Sounds pretty stupid, huh?"

"Well, it depends, . . . are you for them or against them?" Jack asked, opening the door to their classroom.

"I'm not sure yet. Do you have an opinion you'd like to share on the subject?"

"I've got an opinion," Mike Tucker said, as he came up behind them. "What's the subject?"

"None of your business, Tucker," Jack said.

"Aw, don't be like that, Dawson. You know we can't have secrets from each other. Are we, or are we not, The Three Musketeers?"

"Not," Jack said.

"Stop it, Jack," Laurie said, amused in spite of herself. She patted Mike's shoulder as she sat down at her desk. "Of course we are, Mike."

Mike gave Jack a victorious smirk and sat down at this desk on Laurie's left. Jack glared at him over Laurie's head, and then sat down in his assigned place at her right. Laurie wasn't worried; Jack and Mike were always competing for something.

Mike smiled pleasantly at Laurie, ignoring Jack: "So what are we discussing?"

Jack and Laurie looked at each other: "Apples."

The rest of the morning Laurie was too busy to think much about her situation. Even though Jack and Mike were juniors and she was only a freshman, they shared two of her classes, psychology and German, besides being in the same homeroom. Laurie found it almost impossible to take anything seriously when they were around. Sometimes she thought Mr. Jarvis, their homeroom and psychology teacher, had put her in the back of the room with them just to keep them halfway civilized. She knew the real reason—that she was too tall, that she looked like a grown woman instead of a girl of fourteen, and that she made Mr. Jarvis nervous—but sometimes it was nice to pretend she was just like everyone else, even if she wasn't. Today, more than ever, she wished she could be like Julie Livingston—popular, cute, blond, little, and the star dancer in their ballet class. Correction: no longer "their" ballet class. Mr. Lanier had called Laurie's mother a few months ago to inform her that, although her daughter had talent, he regretted that Laurie's extreme height at such a young age precluded any future as a dancer: no partner would ever be able to lift her. So ended Laurie's involvement in ballet class and her hopes of becoming a famous ballerina.

Until two days ago, it had been a mystery to Laurie how she'd come to be so tall. She was not built like any of the women in the family, at least not like her grandmothers, mother, or her sister Ruthie. Ruthie, much to Laurie's dismay, seemed to be growing into another Julie Livingston, only with auburn hair instead of blond. Laurie's own shade was somewhere between plain brown, as in the wrapper, and dull. Her mother called the color "ash blond;" she overheard Julie describing it one day as "the color of dirty dishwater." Julie knew her colors: she also excelled in art.

Laurie moved through the cafeteria line, refusing to glance at the fat-laden macaroni and cheese, which she loved but did not dare touch. She took a green salad and a carton of milk, ignored the desserts, paid the cashier, and looked for somewhere unobtrusive to sit. Julie, holding court with her admirers, sat next to the patio windows. Laurie went in the opposite direction to a small empty table behind a pillar where she could sit unobserved. She told herself she preferred being by herself, but the truth was that today she would've liked to have had a friend to talk to . . .

"Oh, stop it, Laurie," she said to herself. "Save it for the stage." She emptied her tray and sat down to her lunch.

When Laurie saw Jack and Mike approaching a few minutes later, she'd changed her mind about wanting to talk to someone. All she wanted now was to be left alone.

"Think we should bother her?" Mike asked in a baritone that needed no amplification. Out of the corner of her eye, Laurie saw him nudge Jack in the ribs and nod in her direction.

Please, Jack, say no for me. I want to be alone. Her hopes fell as she heard Jack's reply: "Sure, why not?"

Her shoulders tensed as the boys came nearer. She stared into her untouched salad, praying that they would get the hint and leave her in peace.

"Smart move. If I were you, I'd just let it sit there. There are some heavy rumors going round about the food in this place."

"What?" Mike's voice startled her: she'd been so sure Jack would pick up on her mood.

"Get a grip, Billings. It's us," Mike said, plunking his tray down across from her and sitting. "We decided you needed company, and no one's better company than we are. Right, Dawson?"

"Usually, but maybe Laurie isn't in the mood for company right now."

Laurie looked at Jack and gave up: "No, it's all right. Sit down, will you? I'm getting a crick in my neck."

"See, Dawson, what did I tell you?" Mike said. "She's over-whelmed by our presence."

"Right." Jack rolled his eyes and sat down. "Listen, Laurie, I just want you to know this was all Mike's idea, not mine. If you want us to leave you alone, you've got to be brutal. Mike doesn't understand subtle."

Laurie glanced at Mike, as if he belonged in a cage, then spoke to Jack in a stage whisper: "I know."

"Come on, guys. Lay off. I was just trying to be nice."

"Aw, poor Mikey," Laurie said, drawing the words out and reaching across the table to pat his hand. "Jack, we've hurt his feelings."

Jack looked at Mike: "Not a chance."

Mike sat straight up, disgusted: "All right for you guys. See if I ever try to cheer you up again, Miz Billings." He picked up a huge, greasy taco and took a decided chomp. "Ow!"

Jack and Laurie burst out laughing.

"Hey, it's not funny. I think I bit clear through my cheek." Mike tilted his face up close to Jack's. "Is it bleeding?"

"Not yet, but if you don't get your face out of mine, pronto, it will be."

Mike retreated a bit.

"And for God's sake," Jack continued, "wipe the grease off your mouth. You're disgusting!"

"I know," Mike said with a satisfied smirk. "It's why you love—"

Jack stuffed his wadded napkin into Mike's mouth.

"Now, maybe we can eat in peace," Jack said, but Laurie was laughing too hard to hear.

The rest of the day flew by for Laurie. Jack and Mike never gave her enough time between jokes to get down again. By the end of classes, she'd almost forgotten that everything had changed.

CHAPTER 6
Sidetracked

ALMOST FORGOTTEN IS NOT THE same thing as forgotten and bears no resemblance whatsoever to forgotten completely. Almost forgotten is a memory pushed to the back of the mind, where, like a container of leftovers shoved to the back of the refrigerator, it sooner or later becomes impossible to ignore. As long as Jack and Mike kept her attention on other things, Laurie could almost forget that she'd ever seen the box in the attic, that the man she called "Daddy" wasn't her father, that she'd been born somebody else—somebody whose last name was Lightman. But when their distractions ceased, tiny points of anger flashed in her mind like warning lights.

The short walk to her house after school stretched and gave her much too much time to think, to feel. She wanted to hit the reverse button and rewind her life back to Saturday morning, before she'd seen the box under the bed. This time, she thought, she'd simply choose not to open the box and opt for Nana's old costumes instead.

A horn's blast behind her made her jump.

"Hey, Billings!"

Laurie turned to see Mike Tucker pull over to the curb in his new, blue, 1961 Mustang. Mike's was the only one she'd seen in town.

"Want a ride?" Mike shouted.

Laurie walked over to the car.

"No, thanks. I just live down the next block."

"How about coming with me to the Brick? I'll even spring for a Coke or something." His voice sounded hopeful.

"I really should be getting home. I've got tons of homework." *Actually,* she thought, *the last place in the world I want to be is home, and I couldn't care less about doing my homework today, so be a real friend, Mike, and talk me into going with you.*

"So what else is new?" Mike leaned over in the seat and opened the passenger side door. "Come on, get in. I promise I'll get you home at a reasonable hour. If you like, I'll even help you with your algebra."

"Now *that's* an offer I can't pass up," Laurie said, getting into the front seat.

"Great!" Mike shifted gears and pulled into the stream of traffic.

In a few minutes they were on Brookside Drive, heading toward the drive-in hamburger joint known by every teenager on the northwest side of the city as the Brick. The Brick had two main attractions: the burgers were great, and there was always someone you knew or wanted to know parked in the car next to you. It was, for the high school crowd at least, *the* place to see and be seen. Until this moment, Laurie had gone to the Brick only with her parents—a disgrace she'd managed to hide, because her parents merely drove through and took the food home to eat. Laurie knew that even Julie Livingston would envy her showing up at the Brick with Mike Tucker in his new Mustang. Mike might act like a fool around her and Jack, but to the rest of the high school, he was Mister Cool.

Laurie rested her head against the seat and shut her eyes: running into Julie at the Brick might even salvage the day. A vision of her mother waiting for her at home pushed itself into the fore-front of her mind. I should have stopped at the house and let her know where I was going, Laurie thought, as a tiny twinge of guilt pinched her stomach. *Right. Like she'd really have let me go if I had.*

"You're a real magpie today, aren't you?" Mike said, interrupting her thoughts. "Yep, you've just about talked my ear off since you got into the car. Sure wish you'd shut up for awhile."

Laurie opened her eyes and sat up straighter in her seat.

"Sorry," she said, flashing Mike what she hoped was a dazzling smile. "Actually, I was just thinking how glad I am that you asked me to come."

"Exactly what you should've been thinking." He paused for a moment, and then said in an exaggerated, imitation-of-someone-suave voice: "You know, Billings, . . . I don't just ask everyone to join me for a Coke . . . especially at the Brick . . . and just about never on Mondays." He raised his right eyebrow meaningfully, then winked.

This last was too much for Laurie, and she burst into laughter: "Stop! You'll make my stomach hurt."

"Honestly, Billings, get a grip," Mike said, his voice dripping with mock condescension, "Please, consider where you are."

And with this last, he turned into the order lane at the Brick.

They pulled in behind a big, green Ventura that appeared to be stuffed with teenage girls a bit older than Laurie. Two of the girls in the backseat evidently spotted Mike and started waving. Laurie saw one of the girls point at her and then say something to the driver who started messing with her rearview mirror.

"Do you know them?" Laurie turned in her seat, so that her back was against the door, and she could see Mike's face better.

"Who?"

"Who else? The girls in the car in front of us whose arms are falling off from waving so hard at you."

"Oh. They're just some girls."

The line of cars moved a bit, and Mike pulled the car alongside the order menu.

"Better decide what you want."

"I'll just have a medium Coke."

"That's all? I'm going to have a burger, so if you want more, speak now."

"No thanks, just a Coke."

Mike shook his head.

"Can I take your order, sir?" said a male voice from the speaker.

"You bet." Mike leaned out of the window and shouted into the speaker: "Two number ones with double sauce and pickles, a large order of fries, one medium Coke—you're sure you don't want anything else (Laurie nodded)? And one large Coke."

"That's two number ones with double sauce and pickles, one large fry, and one medium and one large Coke?"

"You got it."

"Anything else, sir?"

Mike glanced at Laurie: "Make that *two* large fries." Mike's head came back into the car.

"Thank you. Please drive up to the window."

"Right," Mike said, more to himself than to the speaker. "I'll get there just as soon as the six cars in front of me get out of the way. Have you noticed, Billings, how stupid some of the things people say to one another are?"

Laurie didn't answer, just smiled in Mike's direction, but she knew what he meant.

"Is there something bugging you or what?" Mike asked, as he shifted out of neutral into first gear and moved ahead five feet before having to stop again.

"What do you mean?"

"I mean, I've never seen you this quiet for this long—never," Mike said without a trace of sarcasm. "So what's the deal, Billings? What gives?"

"I've been talking. I believe I just asked you who those girls—"

"Don't try to sidetrack me with girls. I'm not interested—"

"Since when? That's certainly not what *I've* heard—"

"And just what have you heard?"

"I don't think we ought to get into that, do you?"

"Why not? I have nothing to hide."

"OK, just who are those girls in front of us, and why is the driver constantly staring into her rearview mirror?"

"Just some girls I've seen around school, no big deal." Mike looked at the car in question, then back at Laurie and grinned broadly. "I get it. It's you, not me, they're interested in. They're wondering who you are and where you came from. Don't you get it, Billings?"

"Did you used to date one of them or something?"

"Those dingbats? I have better taste, thank you. No, they're interested in you, because you're the competition, and they're checking you out."

"Competition? For what?"

"For any guy here that might see you and think you're cuter than any of them."

"Get serious," Laurie said, but she blushed at the thought.

She didn't know if Mike was paying her a compliment, or merely saying what he thought the girls were thinking. At any rate, being considered competition, not to say *serious* competition, by other girls had never happened to her before. Certainly the boys she knew had never been interested in her. At five-nine she was always too tall for most of the guys her age, whose eyes had been just about bust high for the last three years and who were not yet old enough to consider that an advantage. A thought occurred to her that all of the guys in her freshman class seemed to be growing. Jack and Mike were only two years older, and she was much shorter than they. Maybe she wasn't going to be so conspicuously tall in high school. Maybe one of these days, she really might be a threat.

"Hey, Billings, the way those girls think, if I were you—or any decent-looking girl for that matter—I'd watch my back. Especially here, where they roam in packs," Mike became Boris Karloff and started inching toward her, "and hunt for fresh young females … to DESTROY (maniacal laugh) them—"

"Knock it off, Boris, and drive," Laurie said, laughing. "You're holding up the line, and I'm hungry."

Mike slapped his knee and straightened up: "I knew it! A medium Coke, ha!"

But he was wrong. Laurie didn't want to blow her image—if she had one—by stuffing her face in front of the Brick crowd, so she stayed with her medium Coke and turned down the burger and fries Mike offered, as they sat in the drive-in's parking lot and talked, mainly about nothing and algebra.

By the time Mike started the car to leave, her math homework was finished and, surprise, she actually understood it. What she didn't understand was why Mike had asked her to the Brick in the first place. It seemed out of character for him somehow. Whatever his reasons, Laurie was grateful: he'd managed to keep her mind off her problems, and he'd treated her to a Coke at the Brick. She wondered if she should consider this a date of some kind. She looked at Mike as he turned onto the side street that led to her house and wondered what Mike thought it was. Since she didn't ask, and he didn't volunteer the answer, the matter was still a mystery when they arrived at her home.

CHAPTER 7

Things Unsaid

LAURIE WAVED GOOD-BYE, AS MIKE backed out of her driveway. She watched his Mustang until it rounded the corner and passed out of view before turning toward her own front door. The last few rays of the autumn sun blinded her briefly, so it was only when she shielded her eyes with her hand that she saw her mother standing at the living room window. Her happiness left with the sun as it dropped below the horizon. Laurie wished she could disappear, too, but there was nothing to do but go on into the house. She shifted her notebook and books off of her hip and clutched them against her chest, as she walked slowly toward the house and up the porch steps. At the top she paused, took a deep breath, then pushed the latch and opened the door. A few feet in front of her by the newel post of the staircase stood her mother, arms folded tightly against her chest, as if she were trying to get warm or to hug herself. Laurie walked fast and straight toward the stairs, hoping to get past the frowning sentinel before it could stop her.

"Hold it right there," her mother said in a measured contralto voice that Laurie hardly recognized.

Laurie stopped, angry with herself for the automatic obedience, and pointedly stared at the floor.

"*Look* at me when I'm talking to you," the unfamiliar voice said, each word dropping like small rocks into a well.

Laurie whipped her head up and around and glared into her mother's eyes. To her immense satisfaction, she saw her mother flinch ever so slightly and renew her grip on herself.

"I'd like an explanation, if you don't mind."

"For what?" Laurie spat the words: they tasted bitter on her tongue.

Meg's knuckles whitened as her grip tightened on her arms: "For not letting me know you'd be two-and-a-half hours late getting home from school for a start—"

"It's only five-thirty. For crying out loud, Mother, it's not like I'm a baby!"

"Then don't act like one!" The words shot out—a piercing shriek between two straight lines that had replaced her mother's lips—and found its mark.

Laurie, stung, regrouped in defiant silence.

They stood, immovable, and then the contralto voice began again its staccato, measured inquisition: "Just where have you been all this time?"

"Out," Laurie said, knowing its power to provoke. She waited for the explosion.

Her mother stared and hugged her body even tighter, and Laurie saw pain and anger mingled in Meg's eyes, and something else—something Laurie hadn't seen before. Suddenly Meg turned away from her daughter and walked quickly toward the kitchen.

"Go on up to your room and stay there till I call you," she said, not looking back. "I'm too angry to get into this right now."

Jubilant, Laurie ran upstairs and into her room, dropping her books onto the floor beside the bed. This would all blow over before dinner: her mother was incapable of sustained anger. *Besides,* Laurie thought, throwing herself across the bed, *I'm the one who should be angry.*

And with that thought, she was: all the feelings of the past two days that had been carefully held back rushed through her mind in a torrent and spilled over her eyelids and down her cheeks. Boulder-sobs crashed against her breastbone, until it hurt so much, she thought it must be broken. She couldn't breathe, but she couldn't stop crying either. From somewhere outside herself, as if a part of her split off and observed, she assessed the drama of the situation and found it wanting. After all, no one knew how miserable she was, up here in her room with the door closed. Her chest hurt and her nose had stopped up. The sobbing body on the bed rolled over and reached for the tissues on the nightstand. Laurie blew her nose and sat up on the edge of the bed, where she caught a glimpse of herself in the full-length mirror on the bedroom door. Her face looked like rising bread dough—pale, and getting puffier by the second. Her red-rimmed eyes were nearly lost in it. Her ugliness made her cry harder, and she fell back onto the bed, clutching a wadded tissue in her hand.

"Why did you do this to me?" she asked the ceiling and closed her eyes when there was no answer.

⁓

Laurie awoke feeling cold, cramped, and hungry. She had no idea how long she'd been asleep, but her room was dark, except for a long, upside-down-U of light framing her closed door. She lay there for a moment getting her bearings, letting her eyes grow accustomed to the dark. Gradually, Laurie became aware of the mumble of voices coming from somewhere downstairs and the mingled aroma of bread and meat. Her stomach growled, urging her to action. She sat up and turned on the reading light over her bed.

"Laurie?" Ruthie's high-pitched whisper pierced the bedroom door. "Laurie, you up yet?"

Laurie sighed and stood up: "No, I turned the light on in my sleep . . . of *course*, I'm up, Ruthie. What do you want?"

"Can I come in?"

"Not now." Laurie heard Ruthie's disappointment in the silence. "Maybe later. What do you want?"

"Nothing. Momma said to tell you it's time to eat." The floor squeaked on the other side of the door.

"Ruthie?"

There was no answer. Laurie got up and opened her door in time to see her sister's back as she reached the last stair and trotted off into the dining room.

"Swell. Now I'll get it for being *mean* to my baby sister." Laurie controlled the urge to slam the door as she closed it.

She felt better after washing her face. Most of the swelling around her eyes and nose had decreased, and though her eyes were still a bit bloodshot and her eyelids thicker than normal, Laurie thought it wasn't immediately apparent that she'd been crying. She pulled her hair back into a ponytail, tossed her skirt and blouse on the bed, donned threadbare, faded jeans, tennis shoes, and her favorite gray sweatshirt, and galloped down the stairs—the smell of food overcoming any misgivings about facing her mother.

"Decided to join us?" her father said, as Laurie walked into the dining room. "You arrived just in time. I was just about to finish off the meatloaf."

Laurie sat down and passed her plate to him. He was right; there wasn't much dinner left—a few green beans, a dab of mashed potatoes, a tablespoon of congealed gravy and one, lone biscuit. They certainly hadn't held back because of her.

No one else spoke, though Laurie noticed that Stevie glanced furtively at their mother before poking Ruthie in the ribs. Ruthie flinched and wriggled briefly in her chair, but said nothing. It was obvious they'd been talking about her. Laurie wished that her mother would say something, but she seemed more interested in stabbing a stubborn green bean with her fork than in her eldest daughter's presence. Laurie looked at her meager dinner and felt like an outsider. Eric Billings sat at the head of the table, but he was no longer *her* father; he belonged to Ruthie and Stevie, not to her.

"Meg, honey, the dinner was great as usual."

"It's just meatloaf." Meg's voice sounded tired, worn out. "I just couldn't think of anything to fix."

"You know how I love meatloaf," Eric said, smiling across the table at his wife. "You should think of it more often."

"I'm glad you liked it," Meg said.

"Well, Laurie, Mom tells me you had quite a day."

Laurie looked up at him and waited. He smiled, but it looked forced.

"Would you like to tell us about it?"

Laurie swallowed a bite of meatloaf. The muscles in her neck and shoulders tightened. She cut another bite of meatloaf.

"Didn't you hear me?"

"I heard you," Laurie said and put the bite into her mouth.

"Look." Her father's voice sounded like he was trying to control his temper. Laurie looked up at him. "I don't know what exactly has been going on between you and your mother over the past two days, but I, for one, am getting sick and tired of your attitude. Since when do you not acknowledge me when I'm speaking to you?"

Laurie kept quiet.

"I don't know what's going on, but I do know that I'm not going to put up with this. Now, either you tell me what's bothering you, or you can leave the table and stay in your room, until you have decided to behave like a human being—"

"Eric, maybe I'd better talk to Laurie—"

"Meg, I will not be treated like an outsider in this house. I have a right to know what's going on: I am your husband and Laurie's father—"

"No, you're not! You're a liar!" Laurie threw her fork down on her plate and jumped up from the table, knocking her chair over. She saw the hurt and shock in his eyes, but it didn't matter: he'd lied to her, and he had no rights over her at all. She ran out, back up the stairs, and into her room slamming the door behind her, but it never closed, because Eric Billings hit the other side, and the door banged open.

"Don't you *ever* talk that way to me again! Do you understand?"

For the first time in her life, Laurie was afraid of this man who stood filling her doorway.

"Eric!" Meg tried to push past him, but he turned to his wife and gently pushed her out of the room.

"Meg, this is something I need to handle." He closed the door between them and locked it.

"Eric, don't! She didn't mean it!"

There was fear in her mother's voice, muffled though it was by the intervening door. Meg knocked, but her husband seemed oblivious. After a few moments, Laurie heard the sound of crying fade, as her mother evidently gave up and went away.

Laurie's heart pounded: she'd never seen her father like this. He stood across the room, fists clenched at his sides, face red, barrel-chest heaving with emotion. He seemed bigger somehow, alien, and Laurie realized she'd never seen him really angry before. It was not something she ever wanted to see again.

"Sit down," he said.

Laurie sat.

"Now, I think you and I ought to have a talk." He moved toward her, and Laurie shrank into her chair. He stopped and backed up a few steps. He looked around her room, sighed, and finally sat facing her on the bench in front of her makeup mirror. He looked incongruous, this big, angry man, sitting on a ruffled, chintz-covered bench. Somehow it made him even more threatening to see how he dwarfed the feminine furniture in her room.

"What's all this about my not being your father and a *liar*?"

"Well, you're not my father, are you?" Laurie said, trying to keep her voice steady.

"As far as I know, I am. What are you talking about?"

"I'm talking about James Lightman . . . my *real* father."

All of the strength seemed to run out of him. Eric sat there, saying nothing—frozen—as if she'd pushed the freeze-frame button on Nana's movie projector. Laurie's mind raced: she had to press the advantage she had while she had the chance, but how?

"Is that what Lightman is to you, Laurie? Your *real* father?" Her father sighed and put his head in his hands.

"It says so on my birth certificate, doesn't it?" Her voice sounded more confident than she felt. How far could she go without going too far and detonating the bomb that sat on her vanity bench?

"I suppose it does . . . I've never seen your birth certificate." Eric Billings lifted his head and stared at Laurie, "But I have seen and signed the court adoption papers that say you are *my* daughter, as far as the law is concerned. James Lightman has no legal claim on you at all. Do you understand?"

"I understand that you and Mother lied to me all these years." Tears stung the corners of her eyes, and she had to blink. "How do you think it feels to find out that your father is someone you've never even heard of, and that your sister and brother have a different father, and that you're some kind of freak in your own house!"

"Now wait just a minute!" He stood quickly and stepped toward her.

Laurie threw her hands up to ward off the blow she was certain would come and screamed, "Go ahead and hit me! I suppose you have a *legal* right to do that, too, but that won't make you my *real* father!"

The blow never came. Laurie opened her eyes and saw that he had gone. She was alone.

CHAPTER 8

The Back of the Tapestry

LAST NIGHT'S INCIDENT HUNG BETWEEN Laurie and her family like a soggy, black curtain. When she went downstairs for breakfast, her father—try as she might, she couldn't think of him in any other terms—had already left for work. Park of her was relieved that she wouldn't have to face him this morning; part wished he were here, so that she could say she was sorry for the things she'd said. She hadn't really meant to hurt him; she just hadn't wanted him to hurt her, so she grabbed the first weapon that presented itself and hurled it with all her might. Laurie had had no idea how powerful her weapon was, or how devastating. At first she'd felt exhilarated by the realization of her power over her father, but all night long her words reiterated in her mind, seeming uglier and less justified with each repetition.

Stevie and Ruthie stopped their chatter and stared at her, as if she were a stranger, when Laurie entered the kitchen. Meg stood with her back to Laurie, stirring something on the stove. No one spoke. Laurie pulled her chair out from the breakfast table. The legs scraped noisily across the brick floor. The sound seemed intrusive in the hushed atmosphere of the kitchen. She sat down, hesitated, then scooted the chair back up to the table, half-expecting an irate librarian to appear with her raised index finger held perpendicular to her disapprovingly pursed, thin lips.

"Morning, everyone," Laurie said in a voice she hoped sounded normal. "Stevie, will you pass me the orange juice?"

Stevie looked at Ruthie, who nodded, then he picked up the white, plastic pitcher with both hands and gave it to Ruthie, who passed it to Laurie.

"Thanks," Laurie said. She reached for the empty juice glass on her placemat and poured some juice. "You guys are sure chatterboxes this morning," she said, smiling. When they just kept staring at her, Laurie put her napkin in her lap to hide her discomfort. "What's for breakfast this morning?" she asked the air, hoping someone would answer.

Stevie poked Ruthie, who had turned around in her seat, and who seemed to be staring at their mother's back: "Stop poking me, Stevie! Momma, make him stop poking me."

"Stevie, leave your sister alone, " Meg said without turning around. "Ruthie, come help me with this, please."

"OK." Ruthie hopped out of her chair and went over to the stove.

Laurie scooted her chair back from the table and stood up: "I'll help, too, Mom. What do you want me to do?"

Meg looked at Laurie over her shoulder; Laurie's spirits sank.

"I think you've done quite enough already, don't you?" Meg said, then turned back to Ruthie, and in a quite different tone of voice said, "Honey, get the bowls out of the cupboard for me and bring them over here so I can fill them. Then, if you and Stevie want to, you can get the brown sugar down from the top shelf of the pantry . . . where I keep the spices . . . Can you reach it?"

Ruthie was already on the highest step of the stepladder, her prize almost within reach.

"Here, Ruthie, I'll help you," Laurie said.

"I don't need your help. I can do it," Ruthie said, as she grabbed the corner of the bag and pulled. The brown sugar swung down heavily, throwing Ruthie off-balance. Laurie reached to steady her, and Ruthie dropped the bag of sugar. The bottom split open, and brown sugar spilled onto the pantry floor.

"See what you made me do!" Ruthie yelled. "Now it's all dirty!"

Meg appeared at the pantry door. "I thought I told you to let Ruthie handle this, Laurie. Now, see what you've done!"

"I thought she was going to fall off the ladder. I was just trying to—"

Meg's face contorted with anger: "I have no idea what you were *trying* to do, and frankly, I don't care to know. What I *do* know is you've made a mess and spoiled everyone's morning. I think the best thing you can do now is sit down at that table, eat your oatmeal, keep your mouth shut, and try not to do any more damage before you leave for school. Do you think you can manage that?"

Laurie stood there, tears stinging the back of her nose. She was aware of Stevie and Ruthie somewhere behind her mother. But the thing that held her, like some kind of spike through the heart, was the hatred in her mother's eyes. For the first time in her life, Laurie couldn't speak: there were simply no words. Suddenly, someone removed the spike, and she ran—ran out of the front door and down the block, forgetting her books, her purse—forgetting everything but the sound of her mother's voice and the hatred in her eyes.

CHAPTER 9

No Exit

HER LUNGS HURT. A VISION of balloons blown to their bursting point flashed through her mind, and she stopped running. Her throat hurt. She bent over, panting, hands on her knees, trying to catch her breath, while she waited for the pain in her chest to subside. She had no idea how long she'd been running. She looked at her wristwatch: *couldn't be more than twenty minutes. I'd never make it in a good game of field hockey*, she thought. *Boy, am I out of shape.*

She smiled ruefully, remembering her days as a first-string wing on the field hockey team just last spring, when she could run up and down the field for a full half before getting winded. But that was then. A lot of things had changed since her days in junior high. *Now look at me—out of breath and panting—no, I think I'm dying!*

Laurie doubled up and grabbed her side just under the right lower rib. It felt like someone had stabbed her. She duck-walked to the curb, praying no one she knew would drive by and see her, and sat down. Tears streamed down her cheeks over paths already marked by the ones earlier. *If I don't stop making like a faucet pretty soon, I'll have permanent gullies down my face.* The image turned off the spigot and the pain at the same time and made her smile.

But the smile did not linger, for with the pain gone and the tears dried, Laurie had a chance to look around and realize that she was no longer in familiar surroundings. She knew that she couldn't've run too far from her house in twenty minutes—maybe a couple of miles—but in what direction?

"Get a grip, Billings," she said aloud. The sound of Mike's phrase in the air reassured her somehow. She half-expected to look down the sidewalk and see him and Jack walking casually around the corner. "Gee, Billings, you've really lost it, haven't you? The corner, of course!"

She sprang up and jogged to the corner and looked up at the street sign: Sixteenth and Harrison Avenue. Sixteenth and Harrison was nearly *three* miles from her house. *No wonder I'm winded.* Laurie thought about walking all the way back to her house—not that she wanted to return—and suddenly three miles looked like an impossible distance.

There was a bench near the street corner on the other side, and she crossed over to it and sat down. A pole beside the bench indicated a bus stop, and she rejoiced briefly before realizing her money was in her purse at home. She looked at her watch again: she was late for school. She wondered if her mother had called her in sick so the absence would be excused. Probably not. Why would *she* care whether or not Laurie got into trouble at school? It was obvious her mother hated her. Another thought occurred to her; no one had followed her when she ran out of the house. She leaned forward and looked down the street, willing her mother's cream-colored, Chevrolet station wagon to appear. But it did not, and something told her, something in the pit of her stomach, that it would not, no matter how long she waited. What she'd suspected since yesterday permeated her psyche: *They really don't care about me anymore . . . I wonder if they ever did.*

The street was quiet for the time of day. Since she'd arrived, she'd only seen two or three cars. But then she wasn't exactly near a major thoroughfare. Sixteenth and Harrison was a residential section in the older part of town. Huge elms stood on either side of the street. Their branches, intertwined above the pavement, formed an unbroken canopy as far as she could see. The morning sun shone through the leaves, transforming them into gold doubloons, a handful or two of which were occasionally tossed into the road beneath by a passing breeze. Laurie shivered and wished she'd thought to grab a few things before flying out of the house.

A jacket would've been nice. My purse and books would've come in handy, too. One of these days I'm going to learn to think before I act!

She sat on the bench, disgusted with her lack of preparation, and furious with herself, because her lack of planning necessitated a return to her house in the near future. The last thing in the world she wanted to do was face her mother again, but if she went back, there wasn't much hope of avoiding a confrontation.

Nana! I'll go to Nana's!

She jumped up from the bench and began walking north on Harrison. She turned left at the corner of Harrison Avenue and Twenty-eighth Street, deciding to keep to the less-traveled roads just in case—not that she really expected it, but just in case—her mother, or someone, was out looking for her; after all, she'd been gone well over an hour. Besides, the residential roads were usually prettier and quieter than the main arteries. Twenty-eighth was especially pretty, because the Collier Historical Edition (this tidbit courtesy of a bronze plaque on a tasteful brick monument at the corner) had hired a landscape architect to design seasonal plantings for the median which ran for four blocks between Harrison and

Grand. Ornamental pear trees, dressed in their crimson fall finery, lined both sides of the median. Three large plantings graced each median—one at each end and one in the middle. The architect had employed brick walks among bright-faced pansies, somber ornamental kale, various plumed grasses, and multicolored asters. Here and there holly or bright orange bushes with red berries served as miniature hedges behind wrought iron benches. For the person who wished to sit and contemplate nature for awhile, old-fashioned lampposts stood guard nearby.

The beauty of the landscaping and the growing strength of the morning sun cheered Laurie as she strolled along the winding brick paths. She was in no hurry. On the contrary, as she wandered it occurred to her that her grandmother might not be at all sympathetic to her cause, might in fact march her straight back to the unfriendly arms of her mother. She thought about changing destinations. . . . The truth was she had no place else to go. If Nana would not take her in, she had no choice but to go back—at least for a time—to her parents' home. She could run away, of course, but her practical nature would not allow it. Where would she run away *to*? Something told her that just running away, with no firm goal in mind, would simply be exacerbating the problems she already faced and would solve nothing.

Laurie gradually realized she had stopped moving and was standing at the last garden spot on this side of Grand. *Good thing I stopped*, she thought, somewhat amused that her body knew what to do when her brain was otherwise engaged.

On the other side of the thoroughfare was Nana's bailiwick. Laurie sighed deeply, looked both ways to make sure the traffic had cleared, and ran to the center median of the boulevard. There, she paused to check the traffic again, then ran flat out for the northwest corner that began her grandmother's block.

The key to Nana's house was in its usual place, under the empty clay flowerpot, under the potting table, in the breezeway. She let herself in the back door and called out.

"Nana, it's Laurie! Are you home?"

There was no answer, so she put the key back under the flowerpot and went back into the house.

"Landsakes!" Harriet said, clasping her hands to her chest. "You scared the life out of me, child!"

Laurie's own heart still pounded from the shock of Harriet's sudden appearance, so it took her a moment.

"I'm sorry, Harriet. I called out, but I guess you didn't hear me . . ."

"No, I surely did not." Harriet took a deep breath and let her clasped hands relax. "Well, it looks like I survived, and unless I die of a stroke in the next five minutes, I guess no one's going to accuse you of scaring me to death, though Lord knows you couldn't've done a better job, if you'd tried to murder me."

I could've done a better job, believe me, if I'd been trying to murder you, Harriet, Laurie thought, but didn't voice her comments.

"I'm sorry I scared you, Harriet," Laurie said aloud in her most apologetic voice.

"Well, no harm done, I guess—at least, no permanent harm." Harriet smoothed her chef's apron and pulled a clean wooden spoon out of one pocket. "I was just on my way to stir the stew when you liked to killed me."

She turned away and walked to the stove, pulled a tea towel off a rack, opened the door, and pulled out a cast iron Dutch oven. Harriet lifted the lid, using the tea towel as an oven mitt, and sniffed the contents.

"Sure does smell good, if I do say so myself. My overnight stew. Your grandmother loves it, but I haven't felt like making it for awhile."

"Where's Nana?"

Harriet stirred her stew, put the pot lid back on, and shut the oven door.

"Up in her room, I reckon. She was paying bills the last time I was up there."

Harriet put the spoon on a porcelain pansy spoon rest, that Laurie had given her grandmother one long ago Christmas, then faced Laurie: "Shouldn't you be in school?"

"Not today," Laurie said, and walked quickly out of the kitchen door. "See you later, Harriet."

She could hear Nana on the phone with someone, as she climbed the stairs to the second floor. The door to her grandmother's bedroom was open, so she went on in.

Nana sat at her desk, telephone to her ear. She looked up as Laurie entered the room and motioned for her to find a seat.

"Guess who just came into my bedroom?" Nana said to the person on the other end of the line. "That's right. I'll call you later . . . and *don't* worry."

She hung up the phone and addressed Laurie: "Well, dear, you certainly know how to stir things up around here. That was your mother on the phone, and she's worried sick about you."

"You don't seem very surprised to see me," Laurie said, sitting down on the chaise longue near her grandmother's desk.

One of Nana's eyebrows went up: "Should I be? Where else would you go?"

"I could've gone anywhere in the city . . . or out of it, for that matter."

Nana chuckled: "Not without money or clothes. I don't think you'd have gone very far . . . (Laurie felt her cheeks redden). Besides, I think my granddaughter is smarter than that—much too smart to run away from home just because things are a bit confusing right now."

CHAPTER 10

Reaching Out

LAURIE LOOKED DOWN AT HER hands in her lap and was silent: she didn't know whether to be angry or pleased with her grandmother's confidence in her. Did Nana really believe that coming to her house indicated superior intelligence on Laurie's part, or did she simply think Laurie had no other option? Laurie suspected the latter was the case, though now that she thought about it, if her mother and Nana had known she would come here, it might explain why her mother wasn't out scouring the city for her. The thought comforted her somewhat. Perhaps her mother did care about her—after all, Nana and she *were* talking on the phone when she arrived. Nana had said something about her mother being "worried sick," hadn't she?

Nana's words interrupted Laurie's thoughts: "I'm sorry, Nana. Did you say something?"

"I said, what are we going to do about this situation?"

What do you mean we? The angry words flashed through her mind without warning, and for one terrible second Laurie thought she'd said them aloud. A furtive glance at her grandmother's expression assured her she had not.

"For heaven's sake, child, where *are* you?"

"I was just thinking," Laurie said, not meeting Nana's eyes, "that *we* can't do *anything* about this situation . . . can we?"

"I'm not sure I know what you're saying."

Laurie raised her head and met her grandmother's gaze straight on.

"I mean that it's sort of *my* problem, isn't it? I mean nothing's really different for any of you—except that now *I* know what happened. Why should you do anything at all? It seems that my having a father I've never laid eyes on is not something that bothers you, so you see, I'm the only one who has a *situation*."

"I see." Nana paused for a while, then pushed her chair back from the desk and got up. She held her hand out to Laurie: "Come with me; I have an idea."

Laurie took her grandmother's hand and rose from the chaise: "Where are we going?"

"Into your grandfather's room. I think that's where I put it," Nana said, disappearing into the bathroom that connected her bedroom to what had been her husband's after his cancer had progressed to a point where they could no longer sleep in the same bed.

"Put what?" Laurie asked Nana's back, as she followed her into the next room.

"You'll see, if it's still here." Nana started toward the bedroom closet, but stopped and turned back to Laurie.

"Shall we tell Harriet you're staying for lunch?"

Laurie managed a smile and nodded.

"All right, then. Go downstairs and let her know, while I see if I can find what I'm looking for."

"What *are* you looking for, Nana?"

"You'll know soon enough."

Laurie started through the door to the hall.

"Oh, and Laurie?"

Laurie turned around.

"You might give your mother a call and tell her you're staying with me for awhile today, and that I'll bring you home."

Laurie's heart sank: "Do I really have to go back that soon?"

"Just do as I tell you, and we'll discuss the details later. Now, scoot."

Nana was sitting on the bed, going through some papers in an old shoebox, when Laurie returned. She looked up and smiled.

"Did you talk to your mother?"

"Yes . . . Harriet says lunch will be ready in another thirty minutes."

"Good, I am really quite hungry today."

Nana resumed her shoebox search. Laurie paced from wall to window and back again.

"Here it is," Nana said, holding up a scrap of paper. "You can stop your pacing now. Come here."

Laurie sat down on the edge of the bed, where she could see the paper better. Nana handed it to her. At first the handwriting was hard to read, but suddenly she realized she was holding Jim Lightman's address. She looked at her grandmother.

"Do you think he still lives there?"

"I'm quite sure of it."

"Does Mother know you have his address?"

"No. I didn't want to upset her."

"Why *do* you have it? I thought you didn't like him."

"I don't. An old friend of mine was vacationing there recently and ran into him. He works there. She thought I might need to know where to reach him one of these days, and she was right, wasn't she?"

Laurie's mouth dropped open: "You mean you're going to write to him?"

"No. Why on *earth* would I write Jim Lightman?"

"Then why?" Laurie looked at the scrap of paper in her lap. He was real: someone had actually seen him and talked to him. Then it dawned on her and she stared, incredulous, at her grandmother. "You mean *I* can write to him?"

"It would seem so, now that you have his address . . . " Nana's voice sounded tired. "I don't know if I've done the right thing by giving you his address —"

"Of course you have! Oh, Nana—" Laurie threw her arms around her grandmother's neck and hugged her as hard as she could.

Nana held her briefly, then gently withdrew from her embrace, "Now, listen to me a moment, child."

Laurie tried to arrange her face into a solemn expression, but she couldn't stop smiling. She did manage to restrain herself from bouncing on the bed. She wanted to laugh and cry and dance and jump and sing and shout and run and—

Nana reached across the bedspread and took Laurie's hands in hers: "I'm serious, Laurie. You *must* listen to me."

Nana's tone of voice acted like an ice water bath on Laurie, and she froze.

"I want you to *think*, think seriously, about what you're going to do with this information, and how it might affect the other people involved, before you do anything rash."

"But he's *my* father! I have a right to talk to him, don't I? I don't see that it's anybody else's concern. So what if I write to him? He's got a right to hear from his daughter, doesn't he?" Tears stung the corners of her eyes, and she pulled her hands from her grandmother's.

"I'm not disputing your *right* to contact him—don't forget I'm the one who gave you the means to do it—I'm just saying that sometimes you need to take other people's feelings into consideration before acting on your rights." Nana sighed deeply and shook her head.

"Perhaps, I shouldn't have given you his address before talking it over with your mother first. She has some rights in this matter, too, you know."

"He's not *her* father—"

"No, he's not, thank God, but what about him? What about Jim Lightman's rights? Has it occurred to you that he might not want you to contact him? Or what about your father's—I mean Eric's rights? After all, he's been your father, for all intents and purposes, practically your whole life. What about *his* feelings?" Nana reached over and retrieved on of Laurie's hands. "Honey, you simply must take their feelings into account before you do anything . . . If I'd thought you were selfish, I never would have given you his address."

"But if you don't want me to write him, why did you give it to me?" Laurie brushed her wet cheek impatiently with her free hand. "It's not fair to give me his address and then tell me not to use it."

"I didn't tell you not to use it. I told you to think things through before you did anything. Whatever action you take is going to affect you and the people you love for good or for ill. I just want you to know that there are consequences, and to take those consequences into account, whatever decision you make. Will you do that for me?"

Laurie didn't answer right away. She didn't want to be trapped by a promise she wasn't sure she wanted to make. The silence grew between them, until Nana released Laurie's hand and stood up.

"Well, I'm sure Harriet's ready to serve lunch. Shall we go down and see what she's cooked up for us today?"

Laurie got up, too: "Sure . . ., Nana?"

Nana turned in the doorway.

"Yes?"

"I'll think it through before I do anything . . . I promise."

Visible relief washed across Nana's face, leaving nothing but a smile behind.

"Somehow I knew you would."

They descended the staircase together, and for the first time since finding the box in the attic, Laurie felt good inside—and hungry.

CHAPTER 11

A Change In the Wind

NANA OBVIOUSLY HAD TALKED TO her parents before bringing Laurie home. No one bothered her or said anything more about the day's turmoil, other than to remind her to call her classmates and get the assignments for the next day, so she wouldn't fall behind.

She did, saying to the curious that she hadn't felt well enough to come to school, but was feeling much better now, thanks, and that she'd see them tomorrow.

Later that night Laurie wrote several drafts of a letter to Lawrence James Lightman. It was more difficult than she had supposed it would be. Nana was right: her actions might affect more relationships than she had at first realized—regardless of whether or not the letter actually ended up in James Lightman's hands. She decided to tell her mother and dad that she intended to correspond with him.

The next morning she stuffed the final draft of the letter into her purse. Whether or not she actually mailed it would depend on their response tonight.

"Hey, Laurie, wait up!"

Laurie turned around and laughed, as Jack sprinted down the sidewalk to join her.

"What do you do—time this?"

Jack reached her side and grinned down at her, puffing lightly from the exertion.

"I'm sure I don't know what you mean, *Miss* Billings."

"I mean, it seems rather strange that you're always right behind me when I walk to school. One might think that you were *trying* to meet me—of course, *I* wouldn't think any such thing, but someone else might."

"That someone else wouldn't be Mike Tucker would it?" Jack shifted his books onto his hip.

Laurie stopped.

"No, . . . why would it?"

Jack stopped, too, and stood in front of her.

"Look, Laurie, I may be way out of line here, but I thought we were . . . uh, friends."

"So?"

Jack shrugged his shoulders and stepped out of her way.

"So nothing. Sorry I said anything," he said, and started walking toward the school grounds.

Laurie reached out and grabbed his sleeve.

"Hold it just a moment. What's bugging you this morning? What's all this about Mike?"

Jack seemed to be looking at something over her left shoulder.

"It's nothing, really. Let's drop it."

"Don't give me that. We've been friends too long for me not to know when you're upset about something. So tell me already."

"It's just that a few of the guys were saying that they saw you and Mike at the Brick the other day after school."

"And?" She reached up and made him look at her. "And?"

"And nothing, I guess . . . Come on, we're going to be late."

His face closed, and he shifted the books on his hip again.

They walked along in uncomfortable silence for a few moments, until Laurie couldn't stand it anymore.

"Look, Jack, I don't know what the problem is—I honestly don't." She looked over at him, but he was staring straight ahead. A new thought occurred to her.

"Does it *bother* you that I went to the Brick with Mike?"

"Don't be ridiculous. Why should it?"

"That's what I'm trying to figure out. It *does* bother you, though . . ."

Jack said nothing, just kept on walking.

"I thought you two were friends . . ."

"We are."

"Then what's the big deal?"

Jack stopped abruptly and looked straight into her eyes.

"You're supposed to be pretty bright. You figure it out . . . Well, I've got to see Mr. Albright before class. See you around," he said in a tone she'd heard him use with strangers, then he left her standing on the sidewalk and jogged across the grounds to the school building.

Laurie watched him go in amazement: it had never occurred to her that Jack Dawson might like her as more than a friend. She hugged her books tightly against her chest, smiled, and resumed her walk, being careful not to skip.

By the time the first bell rang for homeroom, the corners of her mouth hurt from smiling. She made her way to her desk at the back of the room, trying to keep her eyes focused on the floor. Mike sat in his regular seat to the left of her desk. Jack's seat on her right was empty. Laurie sat down, trying to keep from searching the room for him.

"You lose something, Billings?" Mike said, leaning over and whispering in her ear.

She rubbed her ear.

"Cut it out, Mike, that tickles." She flipped her hair from behind her ear and opened her notebook.

"Ouch!" Mike jerked his head, as if he'd been slapped.

She didn't laugh.

"Hey, Billings, I'm sorry. I didn't mean anything," he said in a contrite tone. "What gives? I thought we were friends."

"You're the second person who's said that to me today."

"Really? Who beat me to it?" Mike was back to his normal bantering tone.

"Jack."

One of Mike's eyebrows went up.

"Dawson, huh? It figures. Where *is* our third musketeer anyway?"

Laurie glanced at the classroom door.

"All I know is he said he had to meet Mr. Albright before class."

"Albright? Must be about debate stuff then. Think Dawson said he'd be out of town this weekend. Must be about that—"

"Mr. Tucker?"

Mr. Jarvis was pointing at Mike with his eraser. The whole classroom stared in their direction.

"I understand that you're probably not interested in my announcements, since you obviously have something else on your mind. Would you like to share it with the rest of the class?"

Laurie saw the classroom door open. Jack walked in just as Mike started to answer.

"Not particularly, thanks," Mike said, smiling amiably.

"Well, then, perhaps Miss Billings would like to tell us what you had to say that was so fascinating."

Mr. Jarvis's eraser now pointed at her.

Laurie felt her face getting hotter by the second. Jack stood by the door and stared directly at her: he wasn't smiling. She felt sick. She tried to say something, but the words wouldn't come out.

Mike stood up, bowed slightly to the class, and said: "I've changed my mind, Mr. Jarvis. I'd love to share our conversation with the class."

Laurie heard the tittering. She wanted to disappear, to be invisible. Jack's eyes riveted her to her chair.

Please, God, she prayed, *don't let Mike say anything stupid.* She knew it was like asking that a fish not swim.

Mr. Jarvis's voice dripped with sarcasm: "Then please do so. I'm certain we're all waiting with bated breath."

"Miss Billings and I were discussing the nature of our . . . relationship and possible . . . weekend plans," Mike said, his exaggerated pauses and gestures implying as much innuendo as possible.

Whistles and catcalls broke out from various members of the class. Laurie groaned and watched helplessly as Jack left the room.

Mr. Jarvis's displeasure was evident.

"In future, Mr. Tucker, please save such discussions for a more appropriate time and place. As for you, Miss Billings," he paused and looked at her over the rim of his glasses. "Frankly, I am surprised by your involvement in—"

Here, thankfully, the first bell rang, signaling that it was time to go to first hour class, and the last of Mr. Jarvis's words were lost in the noise of exiting students. Laurie tried her best to lose herself in the crush and get out of Jarvis's territory and into the relative anonymity of the hall before anyone could stop her.

Jack stood outside the door of her English class. Laurie took a deep breath, put on a smile which she hoped didn't look forced, and walked up to him.

"Hi."

"Hi," he said, but he didn't return her smile. "I wanted to say I'm sorry for the way I behaved earlier."

"No problem."

Laurie looked down at her books and wondered what she could say to dispel the awkwardness between them. She'd never felt awkward with Jack before, and she hated the feeling.

"Yeah, it is."

The second bell rang: English class would start in a second. Jack tossed his head impatiently.

"Listen, how about having lunch with me?"

"Sure. I'll save you a seat in the cafeteria—"

"No, I mean off-campus somewhere."

"How? You didn't bring your car, did you?"

"Never mind that. I'll take care of it. Meet me at the south door after third hour, OK?"

"OK." She could hear Mrs. Willingham beginning class. "Listen, I'd better get in there before I get in trouble, and you'd better get to class, too—"

A grin spread across Jack's face.

"Free period—I'm Albright's aide this hour. See you in German."

"Bye."

Laurie briefly watched him walk down the hall, then opened the classroom door and quietly made her way to her seat.

The hour dragged even more than usual. English used to be her favorite subject, but Mrs. Willingham managed to make even the most interesting literature boring. She lectured in a high-pitched nasal whine and read selections in the same monotonous tone. After awhile the teacher's voice became a mere background hum, similar to the sound Laurie heard when her ears were stopped up—annoying, but no longer distracting—and Laurie could focus her thoughts elsewhere.

She thought about the unexpected turn of events with Jack and Mike and wondered what she should do about it, but she really wasn't sure yet that she understood all that appeared to be going on, so she decided to put them mentally aside and concentrate on what she was going to say to her parents that evening.

⟶

Frau Gunther stood in the classroom doorway, handing out mimeographed sheets of paper to everyone who entered. Fear knotted Laurie's stomach, as she reached out and took the paper.

Great, a test, she thought. *Why didn't Jack say something? I miss one day—one day—and no one tells me there's going to be a German test? Typical.*

On test days Frau Gunther separated the desks so that no one could see anyone else's paper, so students were not in their regular chairs. Jack hadn't arrived yet, so Laurie had no chance to talk to him before the test. Mike waved from across the room and motioned to a seat near him. Frau Gunther frowned, so Laurie sat down in the front row without returning his greeting. Jack came in just as the teacher started to close the door and took a seat somewhere behind Laurie.

The test took the entire period. Just before the bell rang, Frau Gunther informed the class that she'd written their homework assignment on the board, so Laurie had no time to speak to Jack after class either, since she was frantically trying to copy down the homework. She couldn't afford to miss the homework; she knew she'd blown the test. He tapped his knuckles on her desktop as he passed, but by the time she looked up, he was already in the hall. She didn't see Mike leave at all.

Algebra took her total concentration just to understand what she didn't understand, so she could ask Mr. Melbourne the right questions.

Why, she thought, *did they have to make everything so complicated?*

Mr. Melbourne gave out the new formula for the day: $A + B = C$.

Super. The only difficulty was which numbers were you supposed to plug in for A, B, and C? How did you know which was which? She thought about raising her hand and asking, but no one else seemed to be having a problem. Laurie looked at the problem set assigned for tomorrow's homework and sighed. Why couldn't they just tell you what they were talking about?

The bell rang, announcing the end of third period, and Laurie breathed a sigh of relief, as she bent over and retrieved her books from the rack underneath the desk.

"I hear you're dating Mike Tucker now," said a female voice behind her.

Laurie looked up to see who was speaking. A slender, dark-haired girl who looked like she belonged on the cover of *Glamour* stood looking down on her. For a moment, Laurie didn't recognize her, then she remembered: Judy Rhineheart. Judy was a junior and had been up for Homecoming Queen but had lost out to Patti Preston.

Laurie got up, smiled, and said, "Isn't your name Patti? You look familiar."

Judy colored and backed away from Laurie's desk a bit: "No, I'm Judy Rhineheart."

Laurie smiled broadly: "Of course! You were up for Homecoming Queen, weren't you?"

Laurie walked toward the door. Judy stayed beside her.

"That's right."

"Well, Judy, it's nice to meet you. Sorry I can't stay and chat, but I promised to meet someone for lunch."

Laurie started to leave, but Judy grabbed her arm—hard.

"Listen, whatever-your-name-is—"

"Laurie. And you can let go of my arm now."

"And you can stay away from Mike Tucker."

"I don't know where you get your information, and I don't care, but if I *were* dating Mike Tucker, which, by-the-way, I'm not, I sure wouldn't stop seeing him because of you. Now, let go of my arm . . ."

Laurie's voice sounded a lot more confident than she felt. Inside her heart pounded, and she knew her face must be as red as the leaves outside. No one had ever talked to her like this in her life. It was humiliating—like dialogue from a soap opera. Fortunately, no one seemed to be paying any attention. All she wanted to do was get to the south door and get out of the building.

Please, God, don't let her make a big scene out of this!

"There you are!"

The sound of Jack's voice had never been so welcome.

Judy dropped Laurie's arm and immediately became all sweetness and light.

"Why, hello, Jack. I haven't seen you lately," she cooed. "Where have you been hiding?"

"In all the same old places, Judy. Good to see you," he said in a tone that lacked sincerity.

"Sorry to tear her away," he continued, putting his arm around Laurie's shoulders, "but we have a lunch date. See you around. Bye."

And with that, he propelled Laurie away from the stupefied Judy, down the hall, through the south exit, and into the parking lot where Laurie spied his silver-blue Corvair.

"Thanks."

"It was nothing. Slaying dragons and rescuing fair maidens is all in a day's work." He grinned at her and opened the passenger door.

"Hop in, and let's grab a pizza before lunch is over."

CHAPTER 12

Deceiving Appearances

JACK DIDN'T SAY ANOTHER WORD until they got to Dave's Dive, a rundown shack of a place Laurie had heard a lot about but had never been to before. The descriptions she'd heard paled in comparison to the real thing. Jack parked the car and reached across her and pushed open her door.

"Sticks sometimes when I try to open it the regular way," he said. "Go on. I promise Dave's has the best pizza in town."

Laurie looked at the dilapidated old building and remembered her mother's horror stories about firetraps: "Are you sure we have time to enjoy it?"

Jack laughed and got out of the car and came around to her side. He opened her door wider and held out his hand: "Come on. We'll have plenty of time, if you'll just get out. Our pizza's ready. I called ahead. Come on; you'll love this place."

He grabbed her hand and pulled her out of the car. "Trust me."

It was like entering another world. The words that sprang to Laurie's mind immediately were "speakeasy," "Italian," and "Mafia," though if anyone had asked her why, she would've been hard-pressed to answer.

Dave himself looked more like a cheerful, overweight pirate in a chef's apron. He hollered a greeting to Jack as they entered and ushered them to a small, circular booth with torn red leather upholstery where their pizza—which Laurie had to admit looked great—sat in the center of a classic red and white checkered tablecloth. Cokes were already poured into two red plastic tumblers with just the right amount of ice. Two dinner salads sat to the upper left of the matching red placemats. Two large cloth napkins, red, held the utensils.

As they sat down across from each other, Dave pulled out a lighter and lit a candle in a red, net covered, glass globe. Then he smiled beneficently at Laurie and Jack, stepped back from their table, his fingers pressed together over his ample stomach, and said, "Enjoy." Then he left them alone.

Laurie glanced at her watch: they still had thirty minutes.

"Amazing. Do you always think of everything?"

Jack smiled and picked up his Coke: "Not always." He took a drink and set the tumbler down. "Here. Try this," he said, putting a slice of pizza on a plate made of sturdy-looking pottery. "You'll think you've died and gone to heaven."

"You first," Laurie said and laughed. "It reminds me of that poisoned cake Captain Hook left for Peter Pan's birthday—it's too gooey-looking to be good for you."

"Good for you?" Jack took at bite and just sat for a moment, chewing with his eyes closed.

It was too much for Laurie, and she took a tentative bite.

"Oh, this *is* the best pizza I've ever had in my life!"

"What did I tell you?" Jack finished his slice and took another. "More?"

"Uh-huh," she said, because her mouth was full, and held out her plate for more.

"Try the salad. I hope you don't mind, but I told Dave to put the house dressing on ours. If you don't like it—"

"It's wonderful!" Laurie wiped her mouth with her napkin. "But I'm going to go back to school, and no one's going to be able to get within five feet of me because of the garlic."

"Part of my master plan," Jack said, taking another slice.

Laurie sat back in the surprisingly comfortable seat, drank her Coke, and watched him as he ate.

"Do you have a master plan?"

"Huh?" Jack looked up, swallowed, and licked the corner of his mouth before using his napkin.

"Master plan. Do you have one?"

"I might." He didn't volunteer anything else, but there was mischief in his eyes that almost dared her to ask for more.

"Jack, . . . could I ask you something?"

"Sure. What do you want to know?"

He sat back and picked up his drink.

"I want to know what all the fuss is about my going to the Brick with Mike. First you're upset this morning, and then that Judy-person grabs me in the hall and acts like she wants to pull my hair out or something. I want you to tell me what's going on, 'cause I don't have the faintest clue."

"You really don't, do you?"

"No, of course I don't. Would I be asking for an explanation if I did?"

"I guess not." Jack looked at his watch and motioned for Dave. "But it will have to wait, because we're due in class in seven minutes."

"Jack—"

He held up his hand to cut her off and spoke to Dave, who had appeared beside the table with a cardboard box in his hand. Jack handed Dave some money, put the rest of the pizza in the box, and slid out of the booth. She had no choice but to follow him out to the car.

"Jack," she said again, as he backed out of the parking space, "you can't do this to me. I really want to know what's going on. How many other girls are going to come up to me today and want to punch me?"

Jack shifted gears and grinned across at her: "Your guess is as good as mine. Just watch your back."

"This isn't fair! Why won't you tell me what's going on?"

"Great pizza, wasn't it?" Jack didn't look at her, but made a big show of checking the traffic before pulling out into the street. "Thanks for not eating too much. I can have the rest for a snack later. Nothing like Dave's pizza cold."

Laurie didn't know whether to laugh or hit him.

"You're not going to tell me, are you?"

"It sure doesn't look like it." Jack reached over and squeezed her hand. "At least, not right now."

They pulled into the circular drive at the school entrance.

"Listen, I'll call you tonight. You'd better get moving now, though, or Skinner's going to live up to his name."

Laurie got out of the car but leaned back in before she closed the door.

"Thanks for the pizza. It really was terrific."

Jack grinned: "You're welcome. Now get going!"

"I'm going, " she said and slammed the car door shut.

CHAPTER 13

Family Matters

Oh, joy, Laurie thought, as she entered the sixth-hour classroom for psychology. *What a perfect way to end the day—sandwiched between Mike and Jack in Jarvis's class.*

But there was no getting around it: Mr. Jarvis was a stickler for control. He kept seating charts for every one of his classes, even for homeroom, and nobody but nobody sat anywhere other than in his assigned seat, so Laurie reluctantly made her way to her desk at the back of the room. The lunch with Jack had been wonderful, if a bit confusing. The last thing she wanted now was to spark some kind of confrontation.

To her surprise the class went by quickly and without incident, mainly because Jarvis ran an out-of-date film on Freud and appropriated her desk for the projector. Jarvis sent her to a desk in the front row for the duration of the period—"and this period only, Miss Billings." As soon as the dismissal bell rang, she slipped out the door before Jack or Mike could reach her. As much as she wanted to talk to Jack and find out what was eating him, something told her she didn't want to do it when Mike was around. Besides, she had enough to think about this afternoon without having to deal with their problems. She took the back way home.

⌒⌐

"Laurie, dinner's ready!"

Ruthie's shrill singsong shattered Laurie's concentration. She jumped, then froze, as she heard the sound of footsteps running up the stairs. If she didn't do something quickly, Ruthie would be shrieking and pounding at the bedroom door. Something akin to panic spurred Laurie to action. She ran to the door and threw it open just as Ruthie opened her mouth.

"I'm coming!" Laurie shouted, snuffing out Ruthie's words before they left her throat.

The look of shock on her little sister's face—cheeks flushed, eyes wide, mouth puckered, as if she'd just bitten into a lemon wedge—banished Laurie's irritation.

"Hey, pigeon, I didn't mean to scare you," Laurie lied. "I'm sorry."

Ruthie's breath came in little gasps, as if she might start crying—a possibility that nearly stopped Laurie's heart: accusations of baby-sister-molesting would ruin any hope of talking with her parents tonight. Ruthie cocked her head to one side, fixing Laurie with one of her quizzical stares—a primary cause of the nickname "pigeon"—and said:

"You did too mean it."

Laurie laughed and hugged her sister.

"OK, I did—hey, you just about took my head off with that scream of yours. But I *am* sorry I scared you. . . ." Laurie held Ruthie at arms length and said in a very serious tone, "When did you get to be so smart anyway?"

"Oh, *I've* always been smart," Ruthie said earnestly. Then she paused for a second, as if trying to figure out some difficult problem. "I guess you were just too dumb to see it."

Ruthie's dimpled smile returned, and Laurie's heart resumed its normal rhythm. Ruthie galloped downstairs.

Laurie sighed in relief and descended the staircase at a slower pace. *Another crisis averted. I just hope everything works out as well when I talk to Mom and Dad after dinner.*

"But we're not sleepy!" Stevie wailed, as his father turned off the TV.

"Well, it's bedtime for you and Ruthie anyway," Eric Billings said. "Want a piggyback ride upstairs, or do you just want me to throw you over my shoulder like a sack of dirty laundry?"

"Piggyback!" Stevie said, clapping, his tears gone.

"Can I have one, too, Daddy?" Ruthie asked, jumping up and down in her long, granny-length nightgown. "Please!"

"Well, let's see—how about this? I'll take Stevie up, and then I'll come back for you."

"No, Daddy," Stevie said, "Let Ruthie go first."

"I'm on to you, young man. You just want to stay here and watch more TV. I think you'd better just hop on my back and hold on."

Stevie grinned and did as he was told.

"I'll be right back for you," Eric said, adjusting his new load on his back as he spoke to Ruthie, "so don't get interested in anything down here, hear me?"

"OK, Daddy," Ruthie said, her eyes sparkling and her dimples showing.

Laurie listened and watched the scene from the easy chair where she'd been reading and remembered the days when she, too, had ridden piggyback up the stairs on his back. Part of her wished it were still possible; all of her wished she could still think of him in the same way. . . .

In a few minutes, her father returned for Ruthie, who squealed, as he tossed her into the air before settling her onto his back for the promised ride to her bedroom.

Not long afterwards, Eric came back into the den and settled into his favorite black leather chair. The first fire of the season crackled cheerfully in the fireplace beside him. He smiled briefly at Laurie, then picked up the latest *National Geographic* and started reading an article.

"Dad, I'd like to talk to you and Mom tonight about something I've been thinking of doing," Laurie said in what she hoped sounded like her old tone of voice. They hadn't said much to each other since the fight the other night, but then she didn't know what to say to him, other than that she was sorry for what she'd said, but somehow that didn't seem enough.

Her father put his magazine down in his lap and reached for his coffee mug.

"Well, then, you'd better go get your mother."

Laurie stood up and put her book down in the chair.

"But Laurie," her father said (Laurie stopped and gave him her attention), "I don't want to get into another battle this evening. I think we've had enough turmoil around here this week, don't you?"

"I don't want to fight with you guys, either," she said, and she meant it. "I'm tired of fighting; I just want to talk to you and Mom about the problem. I think I know how to resolve it."

"Well, I hope you do. Just remember what I said . . . You've upset your mother a great deal, and I don't want it happening anymore, if you can help it."

Laurie started to yell at him and tell him about how upset *she'd* been, and how nobody seemed to care, but she didn't, and she really didn't know why.

"I can't promise I won't upset her, Dad, but I'll try my best not to."

Eric Billings put his mug back on the end table, then picked up his *National Geographic* again.

"That's good enough for me, pumpkin. Go get your mother. She's upstairs in our room, reading."

Laurie couldn't remember the last time he'd called her "pumpkin," but it belonged to the piggyback days. Somehow it made her feel better.

The door to her parents' bedroom was shut, so she knocked and waited outside in the hall, until she heard her mother say to come in.

The room was lit only by the light of the TV at the end of their double bed, and it took Laurie a second to adjust to the dark.

"What do you want, Laurie?" her mother said from the bed in a voice that sounded so tired Laurie almost left without saying anything.

"Dad said you were reading," she said.

Meg flipped on the reading light over her side of the bed and sat up: "I was. I just decided it wasn't holding my attention, so I opted for an old Bette Davis movie."

"I didn't mean to interrupt . . ."

"For heaven's sake," Meg said and sighed, but she sounded more amused than irritated, "I've seen that movie over a million times. I know *all* the dialogue. I think I can spare a moment or two. Now, what is it you want?"

"I had something I wanted to talk to you and Dad about . . ."

"Is it important?"

Laurie thought about it.

"It's important to me."

Meg threw back the blanket she'd covered up her legs with and got out of bed.

"Well, then I guess we'd better go and find your father, hadn't we?"

"He's in the den."

"Let me get my robe on and find my slippers, and I'll be right down."

Laurie turned to leave, then turned back.

"Thanks, Mom."

Meg was down on her knees, looking under the bed. She came up with her slippers.

"No need to thank me, yet. Let's see what's on your mind," she said, sitting down on the edge of the bed and slipping her feet into the shoes. Then she smiled at Laurie, "I *do* love you, you know. It's what mothers do."

For the first time in almost a week, Laurie thought there might be some hope after all. She practically skipped down the stairs.

"Well?" Eric said, as she came into the den. "Is she coming down?"

"Uh-huh, she's putting on her robe," Laurie said and flopped into the easy chair across from her father's. "Ouch!" She pulled the offending book from beneath her and rubbed her hip. "I'd forgotten I'd left it there."

Just then her mother came in, wrapped in the long, white, terrycloth robe that always reminded Laurie of coffee commercials. She didn't know why; it just did.

"Honey," Meg said to Laurie, as she made her way to the sofa in front of the fireplace, "before we get started, could you possibly go into the kitchen and pour me a cup of coffee? I'm a little chilly."

"While you're up . . . ," her father said, holding out his mug to her, "would you mind warming mine up a bit?"

'While you're up' was normally a phrase that set Laurie's teeth on edge. It was always used when she was neither up nor willing to wait on anyone. For some reason it didn't bother her tonight. It almost sounded like an in-joke that only people in the family understood.

"Nope," she said, taking his cup, "I'll be back in a sec."

Laurie heard their voices as she returned with their coffee but could not distinguish individual words until she was almost in the den. Her parents' discussion stopped abruptly. She pretended not to notice and brought them their coffee, as if she'd heard nothing.

"Thanks. So," her father said, taking the steaming mug from her, "what's on your mind?"

Laurie took her seat in the easy chair and clasped her hands tightly in her lap to keep them from shaking. Suddenly she realized her carefully planned speech had left her, and her heart rate kicked into overdrive.

Please, God, I want this to go well. Don't let me say anything dumb . . .

"Laurie?" her mother said. "Is something wrong?"

Laurie realized how she must look—sitting there knuckles white, head bowed and eyes closed—and she laughed.

"I'm fine . . . really," she added, as she took in their concerned expressions. "Really . . . it's just that I had this all planned out, and all the words just kind of left. Do you know what I mean?"

"No," her mother said. "Nothing like that *ever* happens to me."

"Well, it's awful," Laurie started, then saw their faces and knew she'd been had. "OK, so you know—but now I don't exactly know how to start, you see . . .?"

"How about throwing caution to the wind and just start?" her dad offered.

"OK, but you asked for it . . ."

"This sounds serious," her mother said, shifting her position on the couch.

"Well, it's probably not to you and Daddy, but it is to me . . . See, it's like this," Laurie dropped her eyes and stared at the patterned area rug in front of the fireplace. "Ever since I found out I really wasn't born Laurie Billings—that I had this man in my life, my real father, and I didn't know anything about him—I've sort of had a problem knowing how I fit in—"

"What do you mean, 'fit in'?" Eric interrupted.

"Let her finish, Eric, and maybe we'll find out," Meg said.

Laurie looked up at both of them, but she couldn't tell anything by their faces. She took a deep breath and continued:

"I guess I mean I really don't know who I am in this family anymore—" she stopped abruptly at the expression on her father's face. "Wait a minute . . . please! I really have to say this, and I've already told you my words aren't going to be just right . . . Just listen to me for a second—I'm not trying to be mean or anything, I'm just trying to tell you how I've been feeling, and what I've decided to do about it."

She stopped, expecting to be interrupted again, but they were waiting for her to continue.

"Nana found his address—"

"What? Don't tell me my mother *gave* you his *address!*"

Meg sat bolt upright on the sofa. Her face was flushed, and her hands were shaking so hard that some of the coffee splashed out of the mug she was holding and onto her robe.

"Meg!" Eric said, getting up out of his chair and moving to sit beside his wife. He took one of her hands in his and turned her head toward him. "Look, honey, whatever your mother did she did in the best interests of everyone involved—"

"I hardly think giving Laurie his—"

"Have you ever known your mother to do *anything* without thinking it through beforehand?"

His tone was calm, and Laurie waited, barely daring to breathe, for her mother's answer.

"She had no *right*! This is *my* life she's meddling in now—"

"It's not *just* your life now though, is it? It's Laurie's, too, and, in case you've forgotten, this also affects me."

Her father's words hung in the air like the reverberations of a giant gong. Laurie sat frozen in her chair. Her mother, too, seemed stricken, like someone transfixed by Medusa's glare. No one moved for what seemed hours, and then her mother crumpled into her father's arms and started crying, and the spell broke.

Laurie fought back the tears that stung her own eyes.

"Mom, I'm really sorry," Laurie said, but her mother's head was buried in her father's shoulder, and she couldn't tell whether or not they had heard her.

Despair gnawed at the edge of her mind: the talk was over, and nothing had been resolved. All she'd accomplished was upsetting everyone all over again.

CHAPTER 14

Decisions

⟵⟶

LAURIE SHIFTED UNEASILY IN HER chair, uncertain what she should do next. Her mother still slumped against her father's shoulder. He held his wife and seemed to be staring at something in the next room. Just when Laurie had decided to go on up to bed, her father looked at her over her mother's head and spoke.

"Why don't you tell us exactly what your grandmother advised you to do?"

His remark took Laurie off guard.

"Nana didn't advise me to do *anything*! All she did was give me my own father's—" She broke off. "I'm sorry, . . . I didn't mean to say that."

She looked down at her hands in her lap, then looked back up at her father. Her mother had composed herself and was leaning against a bolster: she seemed drained of everything. Seeing her mother that way gave Laurie a brief glimpse of what her father had meant earlier. Laurie sighed and smiled wanly.

"Why do things always have to be so hard?"

Eric returned her smile, but it seemed a bit forced.

"They're not *always* this hard," he said, and turned to his wife. "Are they, honey?"

Meg's voice sounded thin: "I don't know . . . Sometimes it seems like everything's hard—especially when you think you're doing the right thing . . .

"Laurie, I really thought I *was* doing the right thing not telling you about Jim. You didn't know him; I did." Her eyes seemed to bore into Laurie's own. "Eric *is* and always has been more of a father to you, and much more of a husband to me, than Jim Lightman would ever have been capable of being. There's something . . . *missing* in him."

Her father reached over and took her mother's hand in his.

"Meg, Lightman is Laurie's biological father, and, whatever your feelings are toward him, she has a right to make up her own mind, form her own opinion, don't you think?"

The expression in her mother's eyes was excruciating to watch: Laurie bowed her head and fervently wished she'd never found the box in the attic.

Things will never be the same between Daddy and me again, she thought. *Not ever.*

"Laurie?" her mother said—Laurie couldn't bear to look at her— "Your dad's right. *Do* you have Jim's address?"

Laurie nodded, still unable to face her.

"Well, then, if you want to contact him, I won't try to stop you."

"But you really don't want me to, do you?"

"I think you know the answer to that. *Why* I feel the way I do, though, is a matter between him and me. It has nothing—and should have nothing—to do with your relationship with him, if you want to have one."

Laurie looked at her parents. They sat close together on the sofa. Her father's arm encircled her mother's shoulders, as if he were trying to shield Meg from something.

Who's protecting you, Daddy? she wondered. Aloud she said, "Daddy, what do you want me to do?"

He chuckled, but there was no mirth in the sound.

"Oh, pumpkin, . . . what *do* you want me to say?" He shook his head. "You really want to know what I think? (Laurie nodded) OK, then, I'll tell you . . ." he sighed heavily before continuing.

"When your mother and I got married, you were only ten months old. You were only two months old when I first laid eyes on you, so for nearly fifteen years, I've thought of you as my daughter . . . Of course, I knew I hadn't really done anything to bring you into the world, when I thought about it, but, to be honest, I didn't think of it much then, and I can't remember the last time I did, it's been so long ago.

"I adopted you when you were eighteen months old, and then I was legally your father, but to me the court thing was just a formality . . . So you see, Laurie, when you say I'm not really your father, it hurts. It may be true in your eyes, but it still hurts to hear you say it. It hurts me even more to have you think it. But, be that as it may, I am not your biological father, and now you know it.

"By-the-way, I *do* want to clear up one misconception you have: not telling you about the adoption was not an intentional deception on your mother's or my part. I honestly don't think either one of us"—he glanced at Meg and smiled—"ever thought we were not telling you the truth. It just never occurred to us that you weren't *our* daughter."

Laurie started to speak, but he held up his hand:

"You asked for my two cents, so you're getting a bit more than you asked for, but since you asked, you're going to get it all. . . .

"Anyway, that's how I've felt, and I think how your mother has felt about this matter ever since we fell in love with each other . . . But things have changed now. Now there is this other man, whom you have every right to know, and, frankly, until you do find out who he is for yourself, and what your relationship with him is, you and I can't have the kind of relationship we once had. Maybe we won't ever have that kind of closeness again. I just don't know. . . ." He stopped for a moment.

"You know, I had an advantage over most fathers," he continued and looked directly at her. "Most fathers don't get to *choose* their daughters; I did, and I *chose* to have you as my own."

Laurie felt tears running down her cheeks, and there was a giant lump in her throat that she was unable to swallow.

"Now, pumpkin, turnabout's fair play: I think you ought to be able to do the same and choose which father you'd rather have.

"What do I think you should do? I say, write Jim Lightman. Find out who he is and what you think of him, and of me, then let me—us—know what you've decided . . . Fair?"

Laurie didn't answer—she couldn't without crying—so she just nodded.

"Fine then. It's settled, and I think we all need to get to bed." Eric scooted to the edge of the sofa cushion and extricated his arm from around his wife.

"Come on, honey. Let's get you to bed; you look tired for some reason."

To Laurie's amazement, her parents grinned at each other.

"I love you, Eric Billings," Meg said, and reached over and pulled her husband's face down to her own and kissed him.

CHAPTER 15

Done Is Done

⁓

IT WOULD'VE BEEN EASIER, LAURIE thought, *if they'd just shot me on the spot. What is it about me that insists on following things through—no, I push things through—to a conclusion, whether or not it means the end of me or anyone else? Dumb! How can anybody be this dumb!*

Laurie reached for the covers and pulled them over her head. Sleep eluded her. She'd lain awake, her brain racing, waiting for sleep to overtake her, since ten o'clock. It was nearly three, or so the alarm clock said the last time she'd looked.

Why didn't they just tell me not to write him? she asked herself for the hundredth time.

Because, dummy, they knew you'd just go ahead and write him anyway, if they gave you any flak about it, said the voice inside her head.

"Who asked *you*, anyway?" Laurie said in her makeshift tent. She flipped the covers back down on her chest, holding her arms taut at her sides. The internal voice, the voice of her nocturnal adversary, said nothing.

"All right, you don't *have* to say anything; I know what you're thinking anyway. . . One good thing that I guess has come out of this is that I found out more about—just who am I trying to kid? Nobody's listening to this speech but me . . ."

Tears slid down the sides of her face.

I'll look like a fool if I just tell them I'm not interested in finding out about him anymore. Now I'll have to mail that darned letter! Why do I have to make such a big deal about everything? Why can't I learn just to leave things alone?

⌒

The next morning it took Stevie and Ruthie together to wake Laurie for school. Everyone seemed cheerful at the breakfast table. Laurie barely touched her food.

"Have a good day at school, honey," Meg called from the front porch, as Laurie left.

Laurie turned, forced a smile, and waved half-heartedly.

"Thanks, Mom. See you later," she said, and wondered as she walked down her street, if people on the way to the gallows felt this way.

She rounded the corner and saw the blue mailbox a few feet away. Inside her purse, the letter seemed to throb. She could feel the sides of her purse against her leg throb in response: it wanted out. Like some evil thing possessed of a mind and will, it sat in the darkness of her purse, waiting to be freed, so that it could go about its ordained mission. She was its instrument, not its master.

She stopped at the blue metal box and reached into the depths of her purse. Her fingers found the letter and pulled it out—*Ouch!* A paper-thin line of blood showed between her ring finger and pinky where it had cut her. She pulled the door of the box down and dropped the thing into the mail below. She let go; the door slammed shut. One second later she realized that she didn't want the letter mailed. She opened the mailbox door again and tried to retrieve her letter, but it was hopeless. Reluctantly she let the door close again and continued walking to school.

The weather felt a bit colder than it had yesterday. The light seemed paler somehow, filtered, as if it arrived from some oblique angle peculiar to the season. Laurie looked through the tunnel of trees that lined the street ahead and suddenly remembered what Nana had said about her "Box Theory."

I did have a choice. Nana is at least partially right; we may not choose what comes into our lives, but we definitely *choose how we respond. Like my letter: I chose to write it in the first place; I decided that I didn't have any choice and dropped it into the nearest mailbox. . . .* Laurie stopped walking. *Gosh, people are stupid! I even tried to make myself think a letter could force me to mail it!* Laurie grinned and resumed walking. *I wonder what a psychiatrist would make of that? Humpf! Maybe I don't really want to know . . . what I* do *want to know is whether or not dropping that letter into the mailbox was* the right *thing to do.*

As she crossed the street in front of the high school, Laurie heard the first bell ring. She hugged her books to her chest and ran the rest of the way.

CHAPTER 16

Superficials

TWO WEEKS AFTER SHE DROPPED the letter in the mailbox, Laurie's life started changing, and not for the better. At first she thought it was some kind of divine retribution—God, wielding a massive bat to smash her with. She had messed up, gone against her better instincts, and now God was making sure she paid dearly for it. Nana, she thought, had failed to mention that part of her "Box Theory," the part where if you didn't make the "right" choice in a particular situation, God would punish you for it.

The first change was inevitable: Laurie turned fifteen.

At fifteen in the Billingses' household something wonderful happened: the privilege of having "real" dates was conferred. That meant she could go out, at night, with a member of the opposite sex, in a car (if her date had his license), without a chaperone (not even another couple), until the approved curfew.

Everyone else Laurie knew had been "real-dating" for at least two years, some for a lot longer than that. Laurie had cajoled, begged, pleaded, cried, sulked, argued, and done whatever else occurred to her to do whenever the opportunity to go out with a boy presented itself, all without the slightest effect on her father, the maker and enforcer of the rule.

"It's not going to kill you to wait a bit," Eric Billings would say. "The boys will still be there when you're fifteen."

"But everybody else gets to date!"

And then he would say what Laurie suspected *his* father had said to him—it had the ring of a handed-down, generational thing:

"I don't *care* what everybody else is doing; I only care about what *you're* doing. If everyone else were jumping off cliffs into the ocean like a bunch of lemmings, would you?   Don't be so impatient, Laurie. Your time will come."

And it did.   Five days after her birthday.

"Laurie, telephone!" Meg called from downstairs.

Laurie rolled over on her bed and picked up the receiver.

"Hello," she said, her mind still filled with the plight of the characters in the novel she was reading.

"Billings?"

The male voice sounded vaguely familiar . . . "Yes?"

"You don't sound like you over the phone."

"Who is this?"

"Mike Tucker . . . who else?"   There was a pause.   "I am talking to Laurie Billings, aren't I?"

"Oh, Mike!" Laurie said, as she recognized him.   "I'm sorry; I guess my mind was somewhere else."

"For a moment there, I thought I'd dialed the wrong number . . ."

"Nope.   It's my number, all right . . . What's up?"

"I thought you'd at least recognize my name . . ."

Laurie couldn't tell whether or not he was teasing her, so she thought she'd better play it straight.

"Mike, I'm really sorry.   Your voice sounds different over the phone, too . . ." She waited for his reply, but when silence prevailed, she continued, "Besides, I really was into this book, and it takes me a while to come back to the twentieth century, much less to really know what I'm doing."

"Must be some book," Mike said. "Well, I suppose I'll forgive you this time."

Laurie looked at the receiver and wondered why she needed his forgiveness at all.

"Gee, thanks, Mike. I was worried."

"Look, Billings, I guess we didn't start this out right . . ."

Guess not, Laurie thought, as he paused.

"Listen," he continued, "are you busy Saturday night?"

"Saturday?" Laurie thought a moment. "No, I don't think so. Why?"

"There's this movie playing at the Criterion, 'The Hustler.' I've heard it's great, and I was wondering if you'd like to go with me."

Mike was asking her for a date! Her heart pounded, and she tried to sound normal.

"I'll have to ask Mom, but if it's all right with her, I'd love to go."

"I'll hold while you ask."

"I'll be right back."

Laurie put the receiver down on her bed and flew downstairs. Meg said it was OK, and Laurie ran back up the stairs. She was out of breath, and her heart rocked her with each beat. She took a deep breath and picked up the phone.

"Mike, Mom said it was all right with her."

"Great. I'll pick you up at seven. We'll go by the Brick first and grab something to eat before the movie."

"Great. See you then."

Laurie heard him hang up. He didn't say good-bye. Odd, but then maybe boys didn't say good-bye when they talked on the phone. It really didn't matter; she had a date with *Mike Tucker* Saturday night!

Suddenly she wondered if Jack would call. After their time at Dave's Dive, she'd been hoping he would, but he hadn't. She really thought that her first real date would be with him . . .

Well, unless he calls right away and asks me out for Friday night, he'll be out of luck, 'cause I already have a date for Saturday. Laurie stared at the silent telephone. *It'll serve you right, Jack Dawson, for thinking I'd sit here and wait for you to call.*

Mike Tucker rang the bell precisely at seven o'clock, and it was all she could do to keep from running down the stairs. But she waited in her room for five minutes after her mother let him in, heeding her mother's advice:

"You don't want to appear *too* eager. Mind you, I think it's silly to keep men (she'd really said *men*) waiting too long, inconsiderate, too, but five minutes is reasonable. Besides," Meg had grinned, "it gives us time to calm our nerves, so we don't shake so much."

It had been fun—getting ready, talking to her mother as if they were friends and the same age. Meg had helped with her makeup, and they had gone through her closet, trying to find the perfect outfit for her first date. They decided on a kelly-green pencil skirt, and a white, long-sleeved blouse with small, embroidered violets on the cuffs, collar, and the front placket covering the small buttons, and a thin, brown, lizard belt at her waist that matched her two-inch pumps.

And the five minutes *had* helped.

Mike grinned at her, as she came down the steps. He looked great, as usual, and Laurie felt a thrill of excitement that she was actually his *date*. He wore a forest green sweater over a maize-colored,

Oxford cloth shirt with a buttoned-down collar, the required wheat jeans, and loafers.

"You look terrific," he said, stepping toward her.

"Thank you," Laurie said, but felt happier than she could remember.

"Better get a coat," Mike said. "It's pretty cold out there."

"What about you?"

"Mine's in the car."

"What time will you be back?" Meg said, coming into the entryway just as Mike was helping Laurie with her coat.

"I'll have her back whenever you say, Mrs. Billings," Mike said, "but I thought we might be back around midnight, if that's all right."

Laurie held her breath and shot her mother a pleading glance.

"I think that's reasonable," Meg said, "but no later."

"We'll be back at midnight or before," Mike said, putting his hand on Laurie's shoulder and turning her toward the front door. "Good night, Mrs. Billings. It was nice meeting you."

They drove to the Brick for a hamburger and fries. Laurie was glad she'd brought her coat; it *was* cold in the Mustang. But she really didn't mind. She snuggled into her coat and ate her hamburger, happily aware of several pairs of eyes staring their way from other cars.

During "The Hustler" Mike reached over and took her hand. His hand felt warm and strong and friendly. By the end of the movie, his arm was around her shoulders, but that was as far as it went.

After the movie they went for ice cream at Carnation's. Several people from school were there with their dates, and Laurie glanced around to see if Jack were there, too, but to her relief, he wasn't.

Mike ordered coffee for both of them, along with the ice cream; Laurie didn't want to tell him she'd never tasted it. To her surprise, she liked it, especially with a bit of sugar and cream. She felt like she'd crossed some sort of threshold. She felt older, as if the person inside her five-foot-nine-inch body finally fit it. She held herself more erect and smiled across the Formica table at her handsome date.

Mike brought Laurie home five minutes before her curfew. She stood on the porch with him for a minute and thanked him for the evening. She took out her key.

"I'd better go in."

"Right. It's freezing out here."

Laurie put the key into the front door and turned the lock.

"Well, thanks again. I had a great time."

"Me, too," Mike said. "Well, I'd better get going. I'll give you a call."

"OK. Night."

"Bye," he said and left.

CHAPTER 17

The Twilight Zone

MIKE CALLED THE NEXT AFTERNOON and asked her out for the next weekend. She accepted, relieved that he wanted to go out with her again. She hadn't been a huge fan of the movie last time, but it had been fun being with him, and until he called, she hadn't been sure.

Mike kept calling, but Jack never did, and soon Laurie stopped thinking he might. She was having a good time. Mike treated her like she was the most beautiful, most intelligent person he'd ever known—even at school. He stopped the inane banter, the talk with Jack about the three musketeers. At noon he took her out to lunch or ate with her in the cafeteria.

Jack didn't join them. When she walked to school, Laurie listened for his voice telling her to "wait up." After a while she decided he must be driving to school; she never saw him outside of class. When she did see him, Jack barely spoke. Then she noticed something else: the few girls she'd been friendly with earlier seemed to avoid her. At first she was hurt; then she was angry. There was a brief encounter with Judy, but this time the girl pointedly snubbed Laurie, and Jack wasn't there to intervene. She asked Mike if he knew what was going on, but he just told her they were jealous and to ignore them. Laurie could chalk up the girls' attitudes to jealousy, but it seemed out of character for Jack. Finally, when she couldn't stand it anymore, Laurie followed Jack to his car after school and confronted him.

"Jack, wait up!" she said, and thought how strange it was to be saying what used to be *his* line.

She saw him turn, glance her way, and then continue to his car without speaking. She picked up her pace and managed to catch him before he could pull out of the parking lot.

"Jack, roll down the window, will you? I need to talk to you."

Jack rolled down the window and leaned over in the front seat: "Go talk to Mike."

It was the way he said it that made her angry enough to open the car door and slide in beside him. For a moment she thought he might hit her.

"Fine. I'll go with you."

"You aren't invited."

"That's OK; I'll come anyway." She looked at him and folded her arms across her chest. "Give up, Jack. I'm not budging until I find out what's going on."

Jack turned the key in the ignition and gunned the engine.

"Suit yourself."

He left tire marks, as he left the lot.

Laurie let him cool off for a while before saying anything else.

"Look, Jack, you've been my best friend"—she turned toward him in the seat; he didn't even glance at her—"Actually, for a brief moment at lunch one day, I thought we might be something more . . . Anyway, whatever we are, or aren't, or might have been, I still care about you—"

"Well, you sure have a funny way of showing it," he said.

If he'd used a string of four-letter words, it wouldn't have sounded any worse. Laurie felt like he'd slapped her.

"Jack!"

His name felt like a rock in her throat, and before she knew it, the tears were streaming down her cheeks, and she couldn't say anything at all. She buried her face in her hands and cried and tried to breathe between sobs. She felt the car stop, but its meaning didn't register. Then Jack was holding her and patting her back and telling her it would be all right and that she shouldn't be so upset . . .

But it wasn't all right. Not at all . . .

"So you see why I was angry—"

"With *Mike*, you bet! But how could you believe those things about *me*? I thought you *knew* me, Jack."

Laurie paused and just stared at him, trying to see something in those eyes of his that would tell her why her best friend—her only best friend—would believe that she . . .

"For heaven's sake, Jack! My parents wouldn't even let me *date* until a few weeks ago! How could you think that the first thing I'd do—with anyone, let alone *Mike*—would be to go to bed?"

Her skin felt tight and itchy where the tears were drying on her cheeks. She scrubbed her face with her hands until it hurt. Jack grabbed her wrists and pulled her hands away from her face.

"Stop it! I can't stand to see you hurt yourself like that . . . Laurie, I know you'll probably never understand how I could believe all that garbage Mike was tossing out . . . To tell you the truth, at first I didn't—"

"Well thank you for small favors! How long did it take? Less than two weeks is all I can figure out, and why didn't you *say* something to me? You know, I can't believe that since Mike took me out, *I've* been the topic of this kind of gossip." Laurie shook her head and smiled wryly.

"For years I've been almost invisible. This is a real joke: Laurie Billings, career wallflower, known to be Mike Tucker's—what?— latest *conquest*?" Her voice became a singsong twang. "Well, who'd a thunk it? Imagine, dowdy, old Laurie Billings. Oh, you know—'Miss Empire State Building?' 'Mommy Long Legs?' Mike really must be hard up if he's reduced to *her*."

She resumed her normal voice, "Oh, I can hear it all . . . I'd laugh, if it weren't so unbelievably ugly." She felt the tears welling up behind her nose again; she sniffed and tossed her head. *I will not cry in front of Jack Dawson. I won't give him or anyone, the satisfaction!*

"Laurie, Mike's been saying this since he took you to the Brick that afternoon . . . Why did you think I was so upset about that?"

"I really didn't know—I believe I told you that, too. I thought you believed me."

"I did. Do you really think I'd take you out to lunch, if I hadn't?"

Something mean reared up in her and took over her mouth.

"I don't know. Maybe *you* were trying to score with me, too."

"Is that what you think?" He glared at her, obviously hurt, as well as angry. "Do you honestly think I'm that kind of jerk?"

"Hurts, doesn't it?" Laurie felt her eyes narrow into slits as she said it.

The missile found its mark: Jack gripped the steering wheel tightly with both hands and faced the windshield.

"I think you'd better take me home now," she said.

He did.

The next day Mike wasn't at school. The word in the halls was that someone had "rearranged his face." Within two more days, Laurie noticed that people in school were treating her better; some were openly friendly. Mike called Friday night—he'd been absent all week—and broke their date for Saturday, after he'd apologized for "whatever you think I've done."

After he hung up Laurie found herself just staring at the receiver: he hadn't denied a thing. He hadn't even *acted* sorry— just delivered his all-purpose, "I'm-sorry-that-you're-so-upset" speech with no specifics and no regrets, broke their date, and hung up. Laurie's brain swelled; she saw a brightly lit neon sign over her head flashing, "Tilt!" The theme from "The Twilight Zone" played in her mind, until her arm hurt from holding the phone out, and she hung up the receiver.

CHAPTER 18
Safe Ground

ONE OF THE BENEFITS OF acute depression, Laurie thought, *is that I don't want to eat. I'm* definitely *cuter than I was two weeks ago. I guess I do have something to thank Mike for after all: eight pounds of ugly fat, gone. And, Mr. Tucker, I won't miss them anymore than I miss you—rat!*

Laurie twisted so she could see her back in the mirror.

Not bad at all. Too bad no one's around to appreciate the sleek, new me . . .

There was a knock on her door.

"Laurie? May I come in? I have your clean clothes."

"Sure, Mom. Let me get out of the way, though," Laurie said, and opened her door wide enough to let her mother through. "I'm not exactly dressed," she said, as Meg slipped through the narrow opening.

"So I see," Meg said, smiling at her daughter, as she laid the laundered pile of clothes on Laurie's bed. "Have you been dieting? You look like you've lost some weight."

"Eight pounds!" Laurie crowed, pivoting, so her mother could see the change. "What do you think of the thinner me?"

"Well, don't lose any more or you'll look emaciated—not a glamorous look in my opinion," Meg held up a slightly wrinkled white blouse. "Is this the one you don't want me to iron anymore?"

"That's the one, thanks," Laurie said, and took it from her mother. "It's pretty worn out, but it's great under sweaters." She put it on. "Do you have any of my jeans in that pile?"

"As a matter of fact," Meg said, pulling a faded pair from the pile of clean clothes.

"Thanks. I was getting cold." Laurie sat down on the bed and pulled on her jeans, not without some struggling. "Did these shrink or something? See why I need to lose weight?"

"Laurie?"

"Finally!" Laurie said, zipping the fly with satisfaction.

Meg smiled, "Don't worry; they'll stretch out again."

"Gee, I hope so. I thought I'd lost more weight than this."

"Honey, would you mind telling me what's been going on the past few weeks?"

"What do you mean?" Laurie took a navy blue sweater out of her dresser drawer and pulled it over her head, stalling for time.

"It's just that you've seemed so . . . down, or something. Did you have a fight with Mike? He hasn't been around for a while, and he seemed like such a wonderful boy . . ."

Laurie sighed and plopped down on her bed. She picked up her old, stuffed Ted E. Bear and hugged him to her chest.

"That's the problem, Mom . . . he *seemed* great, but he was just a jerk."

A frown played across Meg's face.

"I thought so." Meg sighed, and sat down on the bench in front of Laurie's dressing table.

"I'm so sorry you had to meet someone like that now. I'd like to tell you that jerks are few and far between, but I'd be lying to you. There are a lot of them in this world, and they are not all males by any means. Wait until you run into some of the female jerks—sometimes they can be even worse than the males of the species."

"You know what I can't understand, Mom?"

"What?"

"I can't understand how you can know someone for a long time, and be friends—at least I *thought* we were friends—and then start dating him and find out he's been . . . well, you might as well know . . ."

"Know what?"

"Gosh, it's so embarrassing!"

"Laurie, what did this boy do?" Meg's face was lined and serious.

"It's not that big a deal now, really—everything's all straightened out—"

"Will you *please* tell me what you're talking about before I go crazy?"

Laurie giggled in spite of herself.

"Don't go crazy, yet. I may need you later."

To her relief, the hardness left her mother's eyes, and the lines around her mouth disappeared.

"Well," Laurie said, "it's sort of stupid, really . . . Mike said some things about me after he took me out, and it got around school and—"

"What did he say?"

"Basically, that I did a *whole* lot more than hold his hand when we were out." To Laurie's surprise, tears welled up and spilled over her eyelids and down her cheeks. She brushed them away. "Sorry, I didn't know it still bothered me that much . . ."

Meg was beside her daughter in a second, hugging her, and making mother sounds: "Sweetheart, I am so *sorry*."

Laurie pulled away and forced a smile.

"I'm OK now, really . . . The thing that got to me—besides having Mike telling lies about me, I mean—was that everybody else believed him . . . even Jack."

"Jack?"

"You know Jack . . . Jack Dawson?"

Meg frowned, then shook her head.

"I just can't think who he is. Have I met him?"

"Not really, I guess. It's just that he's been such a big part of my life for so long, I guess I just thought I'd told you about him. He and Mike sit next to me in homeroom?"

Meg still looked blank, so Laurie added:

"I sit on the back row between them?"

"The one who sang to you that day?" Meg's eyes sort of lit up.

"He's the one," Laurie said, a smile forming as she remembered, "Stood right up in front of God and everybody and sang 'Five-Foot-Two'—it's hard to find a song that says five-feet-nine, you know . . ." Laurie grinned in spite of herself. "Anyway, the thing that hurt was that *Jack* believed the things Mike said, and he didn't even ask me if they were true or not . . ."

"It doesn't sound like he's much of a friend—"

"But he is!" Laurie stopped abruptly and amended, "At least he was . . . I guess I sort of told him off after he told me about what Mike was saying—"

"I don't blame you. I think I would have told him off, too."

"Really?"

"Really," Meg nodded. "Right after I killed Mike Tucker and had his head on a plate."

Laurie giggled, "I think Jack already handled that part."

Meg shook her head.

"You've lost me. I thought Jack believed Mike—"

"Oh, he did at first, but after we talked, he knew I was telling the truth, and when Mike didn't show up at school the next week, the gossip was that someone had beaten him up, and he didn't want people seeing his face in a less-than-perfect condition."

"And you think Jack beat him up?"

Laurie grinned, then thought better of it.

"Well, I don't know it for a fact, of course, but I can't think of anyone else who would—"

"From what you've told me, there could be hundreds of people out there wanting to get their hands on Mike."

"I hadn't thought of that before," she said, and found she was somewhat disappointed.

"So, what's going on at school now?"

"What do you mean?"

"I mean, how are you handling having to sit between these two jerks every morning in homeroom? And don't you have another class or something with one of them?"

"Two classes, with both of them, but they pretty much leave me alone. After I had the fight with Jack, I asked Mr. Jarvis—he's my homeroom and psych teacher—to move me away from them, and, wonder of wonders, he did."

"So what happens now?"

"Now I go to class, and they don't bother me . . ."

Her mother reached over and patted Laurie's thigh.

"You don't sound too happy about that."

"Mike can disappear into the San Andreas fault for all I care!" Laurie looked at her mother, "I just miss Jack. I really thought he liked me."

"He probably does, honey. Don't worry. Things have a way of working out for the best."

"That's what Nana said."

"When did she say that?"

"Oh, I don't know . . . I guess it was when I was upset about—you know, about finding out about the adoption . . ."

"So what did she say?" Meg asked, removing her hand from her daughter's leg.

Apprehension clutched at Laurie's middle, but she steeled herself and answered.

"She's got some theory about God putting people in this box thing . . . and she was saying that the reason you married my father was so that I could be born, and then God sort of worked things out so that he dropped out of my life, so God could bring in Daddy to be your husband and my father . . . She didn't much like Jim Lightman, did she?"

Meg laughed, but the sound wasn't happy.

"No, . . . you could definitely say she didn't like him. . . . Did you ever mail that letter to him?"

Laurie nodded, but didn't meet her mother's eyes, "The morning after you and Daddy talked to me . . . "

"So," Meg sighed deeply, "have you heard from him?"

Laurie shook her head.

"No . . . Do you think maybe the letter got lost in the mail?" She looked at her mother.

Meg stood up, and for a moment Laurie thought she wasn't going to answer, then she looked as if she knew that someone had died, but wasn't going to tell Laurie, because it would hurt her too much, and said:

"Why don't you give it some more time? You've been out of his life practically since the day you were born. Give him some time to adjust to having a daughter again."

"Mom?" Laurie said before her mother reached the bedroom door.

Meg stopped and turned around.

"What?" She sounded tired.

"*Did* everything turn out for the best for you?"

"Oh yes, honey," her mother said, and there was a light that emanated from her eyes. "Yes, indeed."

CHAPTER 19

Compromises and Resolutions

LAURIE STOOD ON A STEPLADDER in the living room, gingerly removing the strands of Christmas lights from the tree. The sharp needles of the Douglas fir pricked her arms and hands, as she reached between the dry branches for the intractable light bulbs, apparently cemented to the twigs.

"The first day of 1962, and I spend it taking down the stupid Christmas tree!" she said under her breath. She yanked on an electrical cord and nearly fell, as the tension suddenly gave way. She grabbed at a branch to steady herself and winced as pine needles poked her flesh.

"Are you all right?" Meg asked, looking up from the living room rug where she sat, surrounded by newspaper, wrapping Christmas ornaments for storage.

"I'm fine, if you don't count the lacerations."

Laurie examined the cord. "Look at this, Mom, " she said, and held out a string of lights, a sap-dappled twig with a faded blue Christmas light firmly attached.

"I'm so glad we're taking that tree down!" Meg said. "Just think how dry it must be. We're lucky it didn't burst into flames."

"But couldn't we take it down some other day?" Laurie asked. "It's the last full day of my vacation . . ."

"I know, but this has to get done, and you're the only one who can help me."

I'm just the only one who will help you, you mean, Laurie thought, as she coiled the strands of lights and tied them at the top so they wouldn't get tangled. She heard her father and his friends laughing and yelling as they watched a football game on TV. *Pretty soon, Stevie will be in there with them, and Ruthie will be out here helping Mom and me put up the decorations. Men are the only ones who get to enjoy the holidays.*

Finally the lights and ornaments were back in the large, galvanized trashcan that served as storage for the Christmas tree decorations. The tree, stripped and pitiful, stood in its bright green stand and waited for the men to take it out of the house. Faded green needles with brown tips were everywhere. Laurie hated New Year's Day. It always looked like a mess.

The phone rang while she was down in the basement, putting things away for another year.

"Laurie," her mother called, "It's for you."

"Who is it?"

"I didn't ask."

Laurie sighed.

"OK, tell them I'll be there in a second."

"Hello?" Laurie said, taking the phone her mother held out to her.

"Laurie? It's me, . . . Jack."

"Oh, . . . hi. Jack, let me change phones, OK?"

"OK."

Laurie covered the speaker and held out the phone to Meg: "It's Jack. Could you hang this up for me when I get upstairs?"

Meg nodded and took the phone.

Laurie ran upstairs to her room as fast as she could, slammed her door, and picked up the receiver.

"I've got it, Mom. Thanks."

She waited until she heard the click on the other line. "I'm back."

"Are you?" Jack said.

"Sure. Who did you think it was?"

"That's not what I meant."

Laurie didn't say anything for a minute. *Why is he calling?* she thought, and tried to tell herself it was probably nothing earth-shattering, but her heart pounded so, she was afraid he could hear it over the phone.

"So, what's up?"

"Nothing. I just wanted to talk."

"That's something new and different," Laurie said, and immediately wished she hadn't.

"Are you really that mad at me after nearly six weeks?"

"No, I guess not. I'm sorry. I didn't mean to sound so . . . well, you know what I mean."

"I'm sorry, too." Jack paused, then continued. "I guess that's why I called, to tell you I'm sorry."

Laurie bit her tongue before the sarcastic retort escaped. Instead she said, "I miss you, Jack."

She held her breath. *Why did I say that? I promised I wouldn't let myself get hurt again.*

"Really?" Jack asked. He sounded hopeful.

This could be a trick, a voice inside her head said. *He's left himself wide open—you can take it back!*

"Really," Laurie said and tried to breathe.

"You don't know how glad I am to hear you say that," Jack said. "I never knew I could miss anyone this much."

"You missed me, too?"

"I've been such a fool, Laurie. I've been crazy about you since Mrs. Randolph made you sit in the back of the room with me in junior high."

"I don't remember that." Laurie tried to think what he was talking about. "You were two years ahead of me. I was in sixth grade, when you were in eighth. We weren't in any classes together."

There *was* a teacher named Mrs. Randolph, but Laurie had never had her for anything . . .

"You probably wouldn't remember . . . It was only for one study hall—you were taking some kind of make-up test, I think—At any rate, I couldn't take my eyes off of you, and you didn't know I was alive." Jack chuckled. "I was pretty short in eighth grade and—well, my mother said I was 'stocky.' She never said I was *fat*."

"You? Short and fat?" Laurie practically choked.

"Yeah . . . Hard to believe now, isn't it?" Jack laughed.

It was good to hear him laugh. All the tension between them evaporated.

"So tell me why I fascinated you so . . ." Laurie prompted.

"I thought that'd get you."

"You were putting me on?"

"No. I've made a New Year's resolution: I'm never going to keep anything from you again."

"What have you been keeping from me?"

"Oh, things . . ."

"Well, that resolution didn't last long!" Laurie laughed.

"OK, but this isn't easy for me, you know. How about a compromise?"

Laurie's defenses popped up: "What kind of compromise?"

"I'll tell you what I'm thinking, if you promise to tell me what you're thinking."

"About what?"

"About us, dummy. What else did you think I'd have this much trouble saying?"

Laurie thought a moment.

"You go first, then I'll decide."

"No fair!"

"Well, suppose you're crazy about me, and I can't stand you, then what?"

There was silence on the other end of the line.

"Well, then I guess I'll just have to learn to deal with it."

The hurt crept back into Jack's voice, and Laurie couldn't stand it another second.

"Oh, Jack, that's *not* how I feel at all, you big dope. Don't you know I've liked you from that first day you walked to school with me?"

"I planned that, you know," Jack said.

"You didn't either; you didn't even know me."

"I told you: I've been crazy about you since eighth grade—nearly four whole years."

"Why didn't you say anything?"

"'Cause you were just a kid for the longest time—even if you did look like some movie star. I had to wait for you to grow up a little, . . . and then Mike came along, and—"

"And I was too dumb to know he was a jerk. I know; I know." Laurie sighed. "Let's just forget Mike, shall we?"

"Deal," Jack said.

"I think I'll make a New Year's resolution, too."

"What?"

"I resolve not to act like a little kid anymore . . ."

"That's it?"

"Not quite. It's a two-parter."

"What's the other part?"

"Yours."

"Mine? How do I fit into your resolution?"

"You have to promise to tell me when I'm reverting."

"OK, but you have to promise not to get mad when I tell you you're doing it."

They were both laughing, when someone knocked on Laurie's door.

"Who is it?" Laurie asked, still giggling.

"Your mother. May I come in?"

"Sure. I'm still on the phone."

The door opened, and Meg poked her head in.

"I know. That's what I wanted to say: you've been on the phone too long, and your dad needs to use it."

"OK. Just give me one more minute?"

Meg smiled and held up her index finger: "One."

"You heard?" Laurie asked, as Meg closed the door.

"I heard. Listen, could I come over, or would you like to go out tonight? I think we have a lot to discuss."

"Hold on!"

Laurie ran to the top of the stairs and called to her mother. "Mom, can I go out with Jack tonight? *Please.*"

"I don't know; you have school tomorrow and—"

"We'll be home early, I promise. And it *is* the last day of my vacation, and I *did* help you with the tree and everything . . ."

"And it's *Jack.*"

"Yeah." Laurie smiled and prayed silently that her mother understood.

"I suppose it's all right. I keep forgetting that you're not really a child anymore."

No, I'm not, Laurie thought to herself, as she dressed for her date . . . her *date* with Jack, *and I'm going to keep my resolution and not act like one anymore, if I can help it. I want to be as special as he seems to think I am. . . .*

That night Jack took her to Dave's Dive, but not for pizza. Instead they had antipasto, veal Parmigiana, fettucini, and coffee by candle-light. Just when Laurie thought Jack was ready to leave, he reached into his coat pocket and took out a black velvet box and gave it to her.

"What's this for?" Laurie asked.

"Why don't you open it and find out," Jack said.

Laurie stared at him a minute, but she couldn't tell anything from his expression. She opened the box.

"Oh, Jack!"

"Do you like it?"

"Like it! It's the most beautiful drop I've ever seen!"

"Then you'll wear it?" Jack leaned forward and took her hands in his. "I'm not kidding around, Laurie. You do know what a drop means?"

"It means we're going steady, doesn't it?"

"Yes, but it's more serious than that—it's a commitment that we're making to each other. I've never given a drop to anyone. You're the only one who means that much to me."

"Could you put it on for me?" Laurie said, holding out the impossibly delicate gold chain with Jack's initials hanging from it like a charm.

She felt his hands tremble, as he fastened the necklace around her neck. She felt the weight of the charm on her chest, and joy filled her, until she thought her body would burst.

Jack helped her with her coat, and they walked to his car. He unlocked her door, but did not open it. Instead, he turned her face up to his and kissed her gently.

"I love you, Laurie Billings."

CHAPTER 20

Waiting

⌒⌒

"So, what do you think, Jack? Do you think he just doesn't care about me?" Laurie asked, as she reached for another gooey slice of Dave's Dive pizza. "I mailed the letter to him nearly six months ago."

Jack Dawson picked up his napkin from his lap and slowly wiped his mouth. He always stalled somehow before answering her questions: it was one of his habits Laurie had come to recognize and love, because it meant he was giving his answer serious consideration, because he took *her* seriously. Jack reached for his Coke and drank.

"Well?" she prompted.

Jack folded his napkin, dropped it on the table, then leaned back in the booth. Laurie had a sudden flash of the future: he'd be sitting in one of those executive chairs—leather, the kind that swiveled—behind some huge desk that could blind you with its shine, and he'd assume the same posture, as he decided the fate of his company, or maybe, even the fate of the world. It was possible: Jack Dawson could be anything he wanted to be.

"I don't know what your so-called father is thinking, Laurie," he said. "Frankly, I don't care what his reasons are for not writing to you. Do you really want to know what I think?"

"Not if talking about this subject bores you, and it sure sounds like it does—"

"Hold it right there," he said, in a tone of voice she'd grown familiar with. It was the tone that said, if you want to have a really *big* fight, just keep pushing, and I'll give it to you.

Laurie somehow knew she didn't want to get in a fight with Jack: in the first place, she'd no doubt that he'd win; in the second place, she hated it whenever she even thought about their arguing. Besides, he was good for her. He knew how to stop her from being manipulative, and precisely when she needed to be kicked in the rear. But the thing that amazed her, that kept her amused instead of incensed at his ability to head off her best histrionics, was that he saw *her*—the real Laurie, the one other people, even her family, only guessed at—and he loved her in spite of it.

"Do you want to hear what I think or not?" he asked again, and retrieved his napkin, replacing it in his lap.

"Of course, I want to," Laurie said, then smiled as she added: "Unless you are going to say something really crummy that I'll hate . . . if you're going to do that, we can skip the topic and switch to something more fun—like us, for instance."

"Don't girls ever get tired of hearing that mushy stuff?" A frown crossed his brow, but Laurie knew he was kidding her.

"I can't speak for all girls, but this one across from you just eats it up."

"Your letter question seems safer somehow." Jack reached for another slice of pizza and took a bite.

"Then talk; I'll wait until you've finished that bite."

"Women," he muttered.

"Just swallow, and tell me what you think—real fast, so it won't hurt. Pretend you're pulling off a Band-Aid. Just do it; you'll feel much better afterwards."

"I doubt that! You mean *you'll* feel better."

Laurie said nothing, but crossed her arms and sat back in the booth and waited.

"OK. I give up," Jack sighed.

"I think there are four pretty good possibilities: one, that he never got your letter in the first place—lost, or something; two, that he got the letter, read it, tossed it, and has no intention of writing you (Laurie winced); three, he got the letter, read it, thought about it, and decided you'd be better off without starting a relationship with him at this late date—frankly, if it's this possibility, he'd go up in my estimation, but I have my doubts."

"Why?"

"Why what? Why would he go up in my estimation, or why do I have my doubts?"

"Both."

"Well, because if he's decided to leave you alone to help you out in the long run, then he's not as selfish as I think he is, because he's thinking of your well-being, not just his gratification that his long-lost daughter can't live without contacting him—"

"That was tacky . . ."

"Tacky, perhaps, but true enough, don't you think?"

Laurie glared at him, but didn't say what she was thinking; she didn't have to.

"And the fourth possibility?"

"That he got the letter, read it, misplaced it, and so he can't write you back, because he's lost your address—"

"Fat chance of that. I *know* he knows how to get in touch with me. After all, my folks haven't moved, and he has to know who adopted me."

Jack shot her a self-satisfied grin across the table: "Well, then, seems like you're back to my first three options."

"Which one do you like?"

"I already told you the one I *liked* the most, but if you mean, which one do I think is the most likely. . .(Laurie nodded)? Well, then, I think one is probably out, because I think your letter would have been returned to you by now, if it hadn't reached the right address. I already told you I'm just not convinced that he's that selfless to stay out of your life for your benefit,"—Jack made a pyramid of his fingers and leaned his elbows on the table—"so, I'm afraid I'm left with possibility number two: that he's a jerk, and doesn't want a daughter he hasn't ever really known coming into his life and cramping his style. I'm sorry, but that's what I honestly think is going on."

Laurie wished she'd never forced the issue. Something in her heart told her Jack's intuition was right on target. He'd been right about everything else . . . especially Mike.

CHAPTER 21

Mending Walls

"HI, NANA!" LAURIE CALLED, AS she pedaled her bicycle down the sidewalk towards her grandmother's house.

Her grandmother, clad in overalls, an over-sized shirt, and a big, floppy hat, knelt beside a flowerbed in which an array of tulips, daffodils, and pansies bloomed. She looked up and waved.

"Hi, yourself. You're just in time to help me with this little chore."

Laurie pulled up alongside the flowerbed and stopped.

"Weeding? Already?"

Nana sat back on her haunches and smiled up at Laurie.

"If I don't start the moment they pop above the surface, I'll never do anything else *but* weed. At this time of year, they're not so hard to pull, but if you let weeds encroach now, they'll establish themselves, settle down, and raise large families, right in the middle of your best flower beds."

"Sounds awful," Laurie said in mock seriousness. She set the kickstand on her bike and prepared to battle the weeds. "Do you have another pair of gloves?"

"In that box over there," Nana said, and pointed to a dilapidated cardboard box, sitting near a redbud tree in full bloom.

Laurie sorted through various gardening tools, until she found another pair of badly stained, heavy cotton gloves, and put them on. She didn't mind helping Nana in the beds today. The late morning sun felt good on her shoulders—warm, like a light sweater. Besides, it was much too pretty to stay indoors and let a day like this go to waste.

Spring never stays long enough, Laurie thought. *Maybe summer runs it off before its season is really up: summer around here is pretty pushy.*

"Are you going to help me rid the world of weeds, or are you just going to sit there and daydream?"

Nana's voice startled her, but Laurie roused herself and walked back over to the flowerbed.

"Spring fever, I guess," she said, as she arrived next to her grandmother. "Do you want me to work in this bed, or start in the next one?"

"Might as well help me finish this one first. I've done most of it already." Nana shifted her position and looked to her right. "If you'll just get those dandelions out from among my violets—is that some *grass* I see in there?"

Laurie walked around to the other side of the flowerbed to the plot of violets, which were just beginning to bud, and sat down on the grass. Carefully, she parted the delicate leaves and peered between them. She nodded her head.

"I'm afraid so, but it doesn't look too bad, yet. I think I can get it all out."

"Good!" Nana said, going back to her own battle with a recalcitrant clump of dandelions, nestled among a plot of brilliant red tulips.

They worked in silence for a while, and Laurie found herself enjoying the quiet camaraderie and the simple task before her. She liked the intermingled smells of the freshly turned soil, the perfume of the flowers, the heavy, sweet pungency of grass and dandelions.

"Gotcha!" Nana said, as she dug out the last stubborn trace of dandelion root.

Laurie looked up and grinned: "Somehow I thought you would."

Nana, her face dirty and sans makeup, smiled in girlish triumph. Her bright, bird's eyes shone under the brim of her straw hat, and Laurie thought Nana had never looked prettier.

"So, my dear granddaughter, what brings you here on this bright Saturday morning?" Nana asked, and slowly rose to an erect posture.

"Oh, nothing, really," Laurie said, pulling a tiny clump of rye grass out from between two violets. "I just wanted to get out of the house and get some exercise for a change. So, I hopped on my bike and rode over to see what you were up to."

Nana rubbed the small of her back.

"Well, I do appreciate the help. Weeding is harder on my back than it used to be."

Laurie shielded her eyes from the sun with one grubby, glove-clad hand and looked up at her grandmother.

"Why don't you just hire someone to take care of the yard and the beds?"

Nana brushed the dirt off her overalls, then looked up at the sky for so long, that Laurie followed her gaze to see what she was staring at. A brightly-colored box kite with long, trailing ribbons flew above them, dipping and straining at the invisible cord that kept it earthbound.

"That's why, I suppose," Nana said, still looking up. "I'd miss small miracles like that kite, if I just sat inside and nursed my back..." She paused for a moment while they both watched the kite dance on the breeze.

"Well," she said, breaking the spell, "I'm parched. Let's go in and have a nice, tall glass of iced tea."

Laurie surveyed the violet border in front of her, then, satisfied that her job with it was finished, jumped up and brushed off her jeans.

"That sounds great. Do you want me to get some mint?"

"You can see if it's up yet, but I don't think you'll have much luck this early."

"I'll look anyway," Laurie said.

"Suit yourself—I like mint, too. And, Laurie, would you gather all of that stuff for me and put it into the box where you found the gloves before you begin searching?"

"Sure. Do you want me to put up the box, too?"

"No, not yet. I may want to do some more gardening later in the day. Just put it there on the front porch, where it's out of sight and out of the way."

"OK. I'll be in in a sec," Laurie said, and started gathering the few tools by the flowerbed, while her grandmother went around the house to the kitchen door.

Nana was slicing a lemon, when Laurie joined her in the kitchen.

"Guess what?" Laurie said, making her way to the sink to wash her hands.

"What?"

"There wasn't much, but I think I found enough to flavor a couple of glasses of tea. What do you think?" Laurie asked, opening her left hand and displaying three small stalks of mint.

"I think you have the eyes of an eagle. However did you see them?"

Laurie turned on the water and grabbed the bar of soap.

"To tell the truth, I almost didn't." She lathered her hands and rinsed them off, then reached for the mint and washed it in cold water.

"I think it's enough, don't you?" Laurie shook off the excess water and held it out to her grandmother.

Nana took the baby stalks from her.

"Plenty, if I bruise the leaves a bit."

Laurie reached for the hand towel and dried her hands and thought a moment:

"Do you remember last year when you told me about your 'Box Theory?'"

"I remember—it's *my* theory but I'm surprised you remember," Nana said, as she carefully worked the thin stalks between her fingers and dropped them into the brewed tea. "Why do you ask?"

"Well, I've been doing a lot of thinking since then—" Laurie pulled a Windsor chair away from the kitchen table and sat down.

"Oh?" Nana went to the freezer and pulled out the ice tray.

"I suppose you know by now—Mother probably told you—that I haven't heard anything from Jim Lightman."

Nana stopped filling the tea glasses and turned toward Laurie, "No, I hadn't heard—I wondered what had happened, but I didn't want to ask. Your mother hasn't said a *word* about it to me. I'm sorry to hear that's the way it turned out."

"Are you, really?"

"Strangely enough, I am. I suppose I hoped that Jim had grown up, and that maybe you and he *could* have some kind of relationship—not like father and daughter; I think you already *have* the best father in the world—"

"So do I," Laurie said, and was pleased to see the surprise on her grandmother's face. She grinned at her. "I guess that's where your theory comes in.

"At first I was so mad at everyone for not telling me about Mom's first marriage, and that Daddy had adopted me—all that stuff. I'd been feeling pretty out of it socially for a long time, too, and I guess that had something to do with it. But the worst part was feeling that my family wasn't my family anymore—that there was really no place where I really belonged, and no one that I really belonged to, except for you, I guess, and maybe Mom. But she was so tied up with Ruthie and Stevie that I felt like I really couldn't talk to her about this—you know, she'd get all defensive and hurt . . ."

Laurie paused to catch her breath. She hadn't talked to anyone, not even Jack, about all of this. Now it was all coming out in a rush of words.

Nana handed her a glass of tea; a slice of lemon floated on top, and Laurie could just make out the crooked green line of a mint sprig. She pulled out another chair across from Laurie and sat down.

"I'm listening."

Laurie smiled: "I knew you would. You're the *only* one I thought might understand."

She sipped her drink; she hadn't realized until this minute how truly thirsty she had been: "Thank you for the tea, Nana. It's really good."

"It's the mint," Nana said. "Go on. I want to hear what you've been thinking."

"Where was I?"

"You were talking about your mother—"

"Oh, yeah. Well, none of that really matters anymore; it's just background, so you'll know how I was feeling."

Laurie looked at Nana's face for a reaction. Nana nodded and seemed quite interested, so she continued: "Well, then there was all this stuff going on at school at the same time . . ."

Laurie told her grandmother all about the situation with Jack and Mike and about the talk with her parents.

"You know, I learned something new about them."

"What was that?" Nana asked. "I thought you said it didn't go very well that night."

"Well, maybe I didn't learn it that night," Laurie's brow furrowed, and she stared at the ceiling for a moment, trying to figure out just when it had been . . . "I guess it just all started coming together, like a jigsaw puzzle, when you have enough pieces put together to start seeing a picture instead of just pieces—Do you know what I mean?"

"I think so . . . go on."

"You know what I really think it is?" Laurie grew more excited, and didn't wait for her grandmother's response, "I think the trick is looking *backwards* instead of forwards. See?" Laurie leaned forward in her chair.

"Not quite yet," Nana said, and smiled.

But it wasn't one of those patient, patronizing smiles adults sometimes gave her when they were trying to be polite, but weren't a bit interested in what she was saying. It was encouraging somehow; the kind of smile that said, "Go ahead, you can do it, just keep trying, and you'll get it."

Laurie laughed. "I guess I'm going kind of fast, . . . but I'm sort of thinking out loud. You don't mind, do you?"

Nana shook her head and smiled that same encouraging smile: "No, I don't mind. I'm intrigued," she said, and sounded as if she meant it.

"Gosh, I don't know if my idea is that great, so don't be disappointed if it's not, OK?"

"OK. I promise I'll just sit here and listen. But you have to promise to stop asking me questions that I feel I have to answer. OK?"

"OK."

"Good. Now will you please tell me more about the backwards thing?"

Laurie took another sip of her tea and a deep breath to help her gather her thoughts.

"Well, I think I mean that when I look *back* at what's been happening over the last seven or so months, it starts to make sense: I see a sort of pattern, like the one you were telling me about on the back of the needlepoint. If you're looking at the wrong side of the tapestry, it'll look like a big mess, but when you turn it over—sort of change your perspective, maybe? Well then, things start to look like someone might—I don't know if I'm ready to say that that someone's God, yet . . ."

Laurie waited for Nana to object, but she didn't say anything, so Laurie continued.

"Well, this someone or something might actually have some sort of plan behind the design."

Laurie stopped for a moment, then grinned.

"I didn't realize what I was saying: I guess 'design' is one of those Freudian slips or something, huh?"

Nana laughed. "Might be; stranger things have happened."

"That's another thing I've noticed lately: Sometimes you—I—say something, and if you really listen to what you're saying, sometimes you're saying a *lot* more than you meant to—but that's another subject." Laurie tilted her head to one side: "Are you *sure* you want to hear the rest of this? Maybe I should go home and write this all down and then present it to you as some kind of term paper—"

Nana choked on her tea, and Laurie had to get up and pat her on the back, until she stopped coughing.

"Laurie, I swear, you're going to be the death of me one day, but I'll die laughing!"

"Does that mean you don't want the term paper?"

"That *means* that I want you to tell me why you suddenly think there's a 'design' in your life, and why you finally think Eric Billings might be a decent father after all," Nana said, all visible smiles leaving her face, "and I want you to get *on* with it!"

Laurie smiled tentatively and began again: "Well, remember when you said that sometimes God puts a person in this box—the circumstances he doesn't have any control over, right? — Nana nodded—Well, that box is there to teach the person what he, or maybe in this case, *she* needs to know . . . Well, with me, I needed to know—a *lot* really, but I needed to know for myself that James Lightman wasn't just kept out of my life, because you and mother, and maybe other people, didn't want him around. Well, at first, when he didn't answer my letter, I made up all sorts of excuses—like he didn't get it, he didn't want to mess up my life—Mom even said to give him some time to get used to being a father again, to having a daughter . . . But then I thought about what *I* would have done in his situation . . ."

Laurie stopped staring at her tea and looked directly into her grandmother's eyes.

"*Nothing* would have kept me away from *my* child. I did a little research about custody matters. You know what I found out? I found out that no one can adopt another person's child without the express *consent* of the birth parent. . . . That means he had a choice, and he *chose* to give me up. Some people make that choice for the good of their children, because they can't take care of them for one reason or another. Later, some of those people regret giving their children up and try to find them again; some children try to find their birth parents. . . . I can't say what happened or should happen in those cases, but I know what happened in mine: for whatever reason, my birth father did not want to be my *father*, and so he let Eric Billings adopt me. And then I found out—by accident?—I'm not sure it was an accident anymore, but whatever it was, I did, and James Lightman was given *another* chance—a chance to explain himself, to re-enter my life in some way, at any rate. And he *chose* not to answer my letter.

"But you know what? Eric Billings didn't *have* to adopt me. He could've *chosen* to be my stepfather, still married Mom, and had Stevie and Ruthie as *his* kids. But Daddy *chose* me to be his daughter . . ." Laurie stopped. Every time she thought about this part of her theory, it awed her. Then she snapped out of it, and laughed it off: "And he even knew me awhile before he got himself into the deal—"

"Does he want out now?" Nana asked, and her tone was quite serious.

"No, . . . amazing, isn't it? Especially after all I've put him through for the last year. You'd think he'd grab Mom and the kids and run for the hills, wouldn't you?"

"I'm certain the thought has crossed his mind . . ."

"No kidding. It sure would've crossed mine." Laurie stopped and rattled the ice in her glass. "Do we have any more of this?"

"Sure. You keep talking, and I'll fix us both another glass." Nana took Laurie's and got from the table.

"Thanks. Talking can sure make you thirsty. It's great tea, though," she added. "Will you excuse me for a moment? Too much tea, I guess," she said, and left the kitchen.

It hadn't been easy, thinking all of this through and looking at herself as hard as Laurie had looked in the last few months. There were some pretty ugly things she'd discovered that weren't fun to admit were there. Jack forced her to see a lot of it, not by pointing it out, but by being the kind of person she wanted to be but knew, down deep where she couldn't lie to herself, that she wasn't. That someone like Jack cared about her gave her hope. He saw something in her that he thought was fine and wonderful and worth loving; he'd even said as much. Through Jack's eyes Laurie had glimpses of the person she might become, the person Jack already thought she was. It was a miracle of sorts that in the midst of her own kind of identity crisis, Jack showed her a person who had existed in her mind only as a dream before. And, because he saw her as that person, Laurie had a feeling that maybe, just maybe, being that other, ideal Laurie was somehow attainable, was perhaps even someone's "pattern" for who she was supposed to be. Thoughts like these boggled her mind and wouldn't leave her alone.

There was another thought that haunted her in the minutes before she fell asleep at night: perhaps, Jack was part of the "Box," too . . .

Epilogue

THE LETTER FROM THE STATE Bureau of Vital Statistics arrived at last, and Laurie tore open the envelope to get the certified copy of her birth certificate needed for her passport application.

"Mother!" she yelled, taking the stairs two at a time, "Mother! They didn't send my birth certificate!"

Meg came running out of the sewing room and met her daughter in the hallway.

"Honey, what *are* you yelling about? What's wrong?"

"Just look!" Laurie thrust the letter into her mother's hands. "They say they won't send me a birth certificate without a *court* order! My birth certificate's *sealed*, or something like that!"

Laurie was shaking so hard, that she had trouble standing. Her heart pounded like a jackhammer.

"I've got to get a passport, or they won't let me go to Germany with the rest of the students. Gosh, Mom, it's July, for heaven's sake, and you know how long it takes to get anything done with the government!"

Meg went to the door of her bedroom and called Eric into the hall and thrust the paper at him.

"What do you make of this? I don't understand."

Laurie watched as Eric scanned the letter.

"It's because you've been adopted," he said. "Hold on a moment; I'll call the vital statistics people and find out what's going on."

He stopped to hug Laurie and reassure her that she would get to participate in the foreign exchange program, even . . . "If I have to get that silly court order for you."

Laurie and Meg waited in the hall while Eric called. They couldn't hear much, just noise, through the bedroom door, then silence.

"Well?" Meg asked, as Eric emerged from their room. "What did they say?"

"Daddy, what is going on? Can't I get my birth certificate?"

"Laurie, when you wrote, asking for the certificate, what did you say?"

"Nothing much. I asked them to send me a certified copy of the birth certificate for Laura Margaret Lightman, and gave them my birthdate."

"Well, that's the problem, you see," Eric grinned. "It seems, according to the State Bureau of Vital Statistics, that Laura Margaret Lightman doesn't exist."

Meg and Laurie looked at each other and said in unison: "What do you mean she doesn't *exist*?"

"I mean, according to our illustrious state government in all its wisdom, there is no such person as Laura Margaret Lightman. They do, however, have a birth certificate for a girl baby, born on the same date to Margaret and Eric Billings, who, coincidentally, has the same first and middle names as the other, non-existent, person."

"Do you mean that they've just made it all up? How can they *do* that?" Laurie asked.

"Well, it seems that when your mother and I petitioned the court for me to be made your legal father through adoption, and had your name legally changed in the process to Billings, your old birth certificate was ordered sealed, and you became my child, just as if I had been in the delivery room when you were born.

"The birth certificate you saw in your grandmother's attic was evidently a copy of the hospital birth certificate, and, therefore, not an official state document at all. . . . I hope you don't mind," Eric added.

"Mind!" Laurie said, jumping up and throwing her arms around his neck. "I think it's great!"

She pulled back from her father and fixed him with her eyes.

"Not only that, but you realize now, that as far as the world is concerned, you are the only father I've ever had . . . and you're stuck with me . . . forever."

THE END

Acknowledgements

I LOVE ALL MY READERS! Even the ones I haven't met yet, but I have to thank a few special readers—you know, the ones who read it before I thought it was viable? So, as always, many thanks to my husband Ed, who read the manuscript, even though he was certain it was a "chick book." Surprise! He liked it; he really, really, liked it. And the best part of that was that he's older than I am, so he remembered a lot of what I wrote about, and it took him back to *his* high school days. Thank you, Ed.

My mother, Mary Wood, read it before she went to be with the Lord, and she—perhaps more than anyone—knew what I was trying to say and loved it. I know: she's my mother, but unlike many relatives of writers, she never actually thought I could write a novel that she would like. I could, and I did—one of the proudest days of my life.

Courtney Briggs, formerly my agent on the strength of this work, who thought it was a "literary novel," and worth her time. Thank you, Courtney.

Jan Lee loved it fresh out of the printer. Thank you, Jan.

Tina Bennett read it after reading *A Defect of Character*, and really wanted me to add more to it. She was taken with the Box Theory. Thank you, Tina. "The Letter" is for you and Aubrey.

Finally, to Aubrey Broughton, my granddaughter, who read it—I wanted the age group represented—and liked it. Amazing. It's always special when you please readers in your own family. She, like Tina, wanted more. I hope I've managed to give you more without damaging the original story.

Finally, to the creative team who helped design the cover and interior and gave some punch to the back copy, many thanks for a job well done.

Author's Note

THIS IS A SHORT NOVEL, I admit, but I felt any additions to this particular story would be superfluous. I had said what I wanted to say from Laurie Billings's point of view. To put in other viewpoints would not have served my purpose. And yet, my readers—Aubrey Broughton, Jan Lee, Courtney Briggs, Ed Hawkins, Tina Bennett, and Mary Wood, to name a few—seemed to want more. (It's nice for readers to want more, instead of wishing I'd stopped before writing the first paragraph.) So I was left with a dilemma.

I may write more stories about Laurie Billings, if there is a call for it, but in the meantime, I thought I'd attach a short story, "The Letter," written in a much different tone, from the viewpoint of a father who chose to leave his wife and children for other reasons than Jim Lightman's. Consider it a bonus, unconnected to this present tale, but food for thought.

Caveat: Since it is written from a grown man's perspective, some language may be offensive, or boring, to younger readers.

The Box Theory, as I've called it, is purely my own invention, so do not blame any theological group for it. The blame is mine, but I'll take it, because I do believe it, and there is more you can read regarding it on my website, "Cogitation_Station" on Typepad, easily reached by going to my main website: http://www.

pamelakayhawkins.com. There is a link to my Typepad blog. Click it, and it will lead you to my longer essays, and therefore to an essay I wrote on the box theory.

The Letter

‿‿

by
Pamela Kay Hawkins

JOE RIZZO WINCED, AS WALTERS slammed in the front door of his room—he let in the light, and light hurt Joe's eyes. He threw his arm over his face and turned over.

"Hey, Rizzo, get up. Got a letter for you," Walters said in his raspy, Jersey-flavored bass.

"Leave it and get out, will you? My head's about to come off."

"It's from a *female*."

Walter's voice reminded Joe of older kids at a playground taunting a kindergartner.

"Who cares? Leave it, and let me get rid of this hangover." Joe pulled a dirty blanket over his head.

"Must be fancy. Letter smells like a damned perfume factory," Walters said, sniffing the letter and making himself comfortable in the only chair in the bleak motel room. "Pink paper, too . . . Who you been hangin' out with, Rizzo?"

Joe groaned, rolled back over, and opened one bleary eye carefully.

"You're not going to let me alone, are you, Walters?"

"Look at it this way, Rizzo; I got a responsibility here. The boss gave me this letter, see?—sort of a sacred trust, you might say—and he expects me to deliver this here letter to you personally. I'll just hang around until you want to get your letter to make sure you really get it . . . Sure wouldn't want *this* one mad at me for not givin' you her letter. You wouldn't want that either, now, would you, Rizzo?"

Walters threw one leg over the torn upholstery. Joe could see the red Oklahoma clay caked on the bottom of his heavy work shoe. Walters held the letter between two stubby fingers, as if it were some rare treasure. With the other hand, Walters fumbled in his shirt pocket for something. He pulled out a cellophane-wrapped cigar, unwrapped it, and bit off the end with his teeth. He spit the severed end onto the stained, worn carpet, reached back into his pocket and produced a match, which he struck with his thumbnail. Walters lit the cigar and tossed the match in the general direction of the garbage can in the kitchenette. He leaned back in the chair, crossed his legs, and puffed languidly on the cigar. It was obvious that Walters was settling in for the duration.

Joe sat up on the edge of the twin bed and ran his hand through the unruly thatch of iron-gray hair. His sleeveless T-shirt, stained with remnants of last night's revelry, hung limply over his shorts. He sat there for a moment, dully contemplating his toenails, and wondering why in the hell people couldn't just leave a man alone to sleep it off.

It had been raining steadily for two days, making it impossible for the road crew to work. There was nothing to do in this wasteland of western Oklahoma but drink when the rains came down like this . . .

There had been a flash flood last night one mile north of where they were working, Joe remembered, that had killed a poor farmer out after a lost calf. Water had come down through one of those ravines. Guy never had a chance. Peters heard about it in town when he went on a beer run. Come back pretty shaken up—young kid, Peters, but nice; he'd never seen a dead man before. They'd brought the old man's body into town just as Peters was leaving the liquor store. Got a good look at him, too. Said he'd never seen a man look like that—must have been thrown up against the sides of the ravine. You get used to news like that out here, . . . but it was a good excuse for another drink. Besides, Peters needed company.

Joe kneaded the back of his neck with his hand and slowly lifted his head. The pain hit like the flood hit the farmer, knocking his head back down between his knees.

"You gonna be sick, Rizzo?" Walters asked, not making any move to help or get out of range.

"Shut up, Walters."

"You really must've tied one on last night, either that or you're getting old . . . Ran into Peters on the way over here. He was sloggin' his way back to town. The mud slowed him down or he'd a been joggin'."

"Shut up, Walters."

"Now you take me, Rizzo. I ain't no health nut or nuthin', but comes a time when a man's gotta start watchin' how he treats his body. What are you now? Fifty-five?"

Joe squinted at Walters through the pain and made a low, growling sound.

Walters grinned and tapped the growing ash at the end of his cigar off onto the carpet.

"Thought so. You and me, Rizzo, we've been around a long time, been through a lot together over the years. That's why I just had to make sure that you weren't holdin' out on your old pal . . . Give, Joe," Walters said, looking at Joe for the first time. "Who do you know that would send you a letter like this?"

"Give me the letter, damn you," Joe said, reaching out his hand towards Walters, but keeping his head down, so the pain wouldn't hit again.

Walters chuckled. The chair springs protested, as he got up and sauntered over to Joe's outstretched hand. He dropped the letter into the upturned palm, then resumed his seat. He drew on his cigar and blew out the smoke in a large, malodorous cloud that encircled him lazily, and finally settled into the fabric of his worn denim overalls.

Joe watched out of slit-eyes, fascinated by Walters's total imperviousness to rejection. The letter lay unnoticed in his hand.

"OK, you win. I'll read the stupid letter, but you've got to leave me alone for a minute while I get cleaned up—"

"Why, Rizzo, I didn't know you was so modest," Walters said, his lips curling up around the cigar into a smirk.

Joe grinned in spite of himself, and turned his head so that he could get a better view of the foreman.

"Look, you S.O.B., I couldn't read a billboard right now, if it was right in front of my face. I told you, my head's coming off . . . I'm not holding out on you, Walters," Joe said wearily. "I think you're building this letter into something big, when it's probably an advertising gimmick of some kind. Hell, Walters, you *know* every woman I do—"

"All right, Rizzo. I believe you. Get up and get a shower or somethin', though. You look like hell. I'll be back later, and you can tell me about the letter."

Walters jammed his cigar into an empty beer can on the floor and left, letting the screen door of the motel room slam shut. Joe's head reverberated with the sound; for a moment he sat there too stunned with pain to move. Eventually, the throbbing lessened enough for him to get up and walk to the bathroom. He moved rigidly, holding his head the way someone practicing good posture balances a book.

The hot pulse of the shower eased his tense and sore muscles and helped clear his mind a bit. He toweled off with a dingy, dun-colored rag, gingerly dried his hair, then knotted the damp cloth around his spreading waistline—the result of too much beer and middle-age droop.

He wandered into the kitchen area: a sink—rust-stained porcelain with a single lead faucet that dripped continuously; a hot plate on a two-foot-long counter of cracked Formica; and a midget refrigerator, clogged with glacial frost, but big enough to hold two six-packs of Coors at a time. Joe opened the door of the fridge, took out a can of beer, and popped the tab top, cutting his finger in the process. Sucking his wounded index finger, he took the six or seven steps to the never-made pile of soiled sheets that served as his bed, and sat down. He swigged the Coors; the can emptied rapidly, and Joe tossed the empty can overhand toward the garbage can. Basket. Pleased, Joe rummaged around in an old army duffel bag for some briefs, found the last clean pair, and cursed that it was time to visit the laundromat again. He pulled on a clean T-shirt with only one hole under the right armpit, and sat staring at the front door, while he gathered strength to finish dressing.

The exertion of movement had tired him beyond endurance, and he decided to recoup his energy by going back to sleep. He lay down on his bed, but something scratched his neck. He reached around and pulled out the crisp, pink envelope of Walters's mystery letter. Joe held it to his nose. Sure enough, Walters was right, the thing did smell like perfume. Good stuff, too, not that cheap, sickly-sweet scent that most of the women he knew wore. No wonder Walters was curious. Joe looked at the front of the envelope. The handwriting was precise, graceful, and totally unfamiliar. There was no return address. Joe propped himself up on one elbow and tore open the envelope.

"August 12, 1976

"Dear Joseph,

"I don't know what else to call you. Dad seems inappropriate after all these years, and Mr. Rizzo is absurd. I'm not trying to be disrespectful—I'm just feeling very awkward and at a loss for the right words.

"I'm sure this letter is as much of a shock for you to read as it is hard for me to write, but I thought the time had come for us to meet, or at least communicate in some way.

"Today is my birthday. I'm sure you didn't remember the date as having any special significance, and I don't blame you for that, but I'm thirty now, and I don't know, maybe it's a magic number or something, but somehow, I started thinking about us—you and me—and how we were both getting older and that we'd really never even met. I thought you might be interested to know something about me, and to know that I am not bitter—that in a way I understand why you had to leave Mother and me. I didn't when I was younger, but I really think I do now. At any rate, I want you to know that I'm here, if you ever need me, or want to see me or anything, and that I'd like to see you, too.

"I got your address from your mother. She and I have kept in touch through the years, though we're not close, for reasons I'm certain you can guess. She was not sure exactly where to reach you, but she said this was your last address, so I'm taking the chance that the postal system can find you.

"Did anyone tell you about me? Did they tell you what I look like—that I'm married? Did you know that you are a grandfather now? My husband, Jack, and I have two children. The oldest is our girl, Janet, and the youngest is Billy, our boy. Janet's six, and Billy's three—he'll be four in a couple of months. My married name is Randolph, and I go by Rebecca instead of Becky. Mother said you always called me Becky.

"I'd like to hear what you're doing now. Mother said you were an engineer of some kind. I have a picture of you taken when you got back from the war, just before you and Mother were married. When I was little, I used to take it out and look at it. I think you're very handsome. Could I have a recent picture of you? (I enclosed a picture of my family and me.)

"I hope you don't think that I'm trying to stir up old memories or anything. Probably this was a foolish thing to do . . . but maybe not.

"Well, Jack's taking me to the club for dinner to celebrate my birthday, and I have to get ready, so I'll close this now. I hope that we can get together sometime soon.

"Your daughter,
"Rebecca L. Randolph

"P. S. My address is: 445 Spreading Chestnut Drive, Darien, CT 06820."

Joe stared at the letter. Something dropped on the page, and the letters of a word ran. He blotted it with a corner of sheeting, then lay back down on the bed.

How long has it been since I've seen her? Thirty years old, now. It can't be that long! A grandfather? She said there was a picture . . . where in the hell is that picture?

Joe reached for the envelope he'd thrown on the floor while he was reading. There was something in it. Carefully, he shook the envelope and a small cardboard sandwich fell out. It was taped along two sides. Joe slit the tape with his thumbnail and a snap-shot fell onto his chest. He picked it up warily and looked into the faces of what was his family.

There was a tall, all-American-type man, dressed in gray slacks and a navy, Brooks Brothers blazer. He had dark hair, blue eyes, and a smile that reminded Joe of a young Jackie Cooper—complete with dimples. He looked like a nice enough guy.

There were the two kids—the girl would probably be a beauty when she grew up. She had porcelain-fine skin like her mother—her grandmother—had, and those eyes . . . Hell, those eyes could swallow a man whole in a few years, Joe thought, a lump forming in his throat. He coughed to clear it.

The little boy . . . what was his name? Joe picked up the letter . . . Billy. Billy looked like someone he knew. He held the picture far-ther away from his eyes, until it came into better focus. *Well, what do you know? He looks a little, just a little, like I used to.* Joe's chest swelled a bit, and then he forced himself to look at Becky.

I don't care what in the hell she goes by, she's still Becky. But star-ing back at him was a woman, a woman who looked so much like Jane that it scared him a little.

Becky had Jane's eyes—dark, brown fawn-eyes—and they stared at him from the matte finish of the photograph, until all Joe could see were Jane's eyes as he'd left that day. She'd been crying for hours—he never could stand to see her cry—but he couldn't stay any longer and still be any kind of man.

Joe looked around his room, really seeing it for the first time, with its filth and darkness, dark mainly because the windows had not been washed since Noah's Flood, and his stomach turned.

Nausea swept over him, as he glimpsed himself in the dime-store mirror tacked onto the wall across from him—some former occupant's idea of decor, no doubt. An old man looked back at him, stubble from three days of not shaving on his face. The dark black bristles were patched with gray, giving him the look of a molting hawk. Joe ran one hand across his chin and got up slowly, letting the picture of Becky and her family drop onto the bed.

He walked into the bathroom and turned on the light, a one-hundred-watt bulb suspended from a bare socket above the medicine cabinet. The light gave no quarter, no softness, and Joe wanted none. He peered into the mirror at his reflection.

Bloodshot, faded-blue eyes stared at him, rheumy and old. It was like looking at somebody else, somebody he didn't know. His hair was unkempt, still tangled from the toweling but clean. Flesh hung in toneless folds around his jaw and neck, and his shoulders had rounded with years of poor posture and stooping over blueprints and survey maps. Kinky black and gray hairs marred patches of skin on his shoulders, while the hair on his chest, visible through the deep U of his T-shirt, was grizzled. His chest sagged slightly, and his shirt stretched over the beer-swollen pot of his belly. Reality in all its harshness stared him full in the face from the lifeless eyes of what used to be a man.

So, . . . Jane had told her he was an engineer. Well, it wasn't a lie, not exactly, but she had meant Becky to envision someone in a suit and tie, with a nice, pristine office, lots of money, successful businessman written in bold type across—no embroidered, in an elegant design—on a silk tie, perhaps.

Janie, you just couldn't tell her, could you? That your husband, the Catholic boy from the wrong side of the social register— 'but with such promise, Daddy!'—was a surveyor, a construction engineer, on a road gang in the Oklahoma panhandle.

I tried to make good, Janie, I really did. Almost made it once, too. Had all my money tied up in a sure-fire oil well, down here in land that oozes oil like Darien oozes money. But I ran out of cash before they hit oil. Couldn't stay in with the guys with the big bucks, so I sold my share for a fraction of what it was worth, and two weeks later, they struck the damnedest oil well in the area. It's still pumping, barrel after barrel, and there's not an end in sight.

That was my chance, Janie. I was going to send for you and Becky then, when I could hold my head up and support you, without having to go to your daddy to keep you in spending money. . . . I just couldn't take working for him. People in the office saying I married you for your money. I know what they said. What dear, old, daddy said about me. The thing that hurt was that you believed what he was saying. I had to leave after that . . . and you wouldn't come with me. . . .

Joe reached for the beaded metal chain that hung from the light socket and pulled. He walked into his room, opened the closet door, and looked in. There, still in the plastic cover from the cleaners, hung his one remaining suit—out of date, now, but then he never had call to put it on anymore, so what did it matter? He reached past the suit and took out a freshly laundered work shirt and a pressed pair of jeans, the ones he usually saved for special occasions like the bar in Woodward with the classy, old-fashioned nude in a painting behind the back counter.

Woodward wasn't that far away, and what if it was only Wednesday? Shelly didn't work on Wednesdays.

Maybe I'll call her up and take her out on the town tonight.

The thought cheered him, as he laid the pants and shirt, still on their hangers, on the back of the overstuffed chair.

Hell, I'm not so old. Shelly's a real looker, he thought, walking back into the bathroom and taking his razor out of the medicine cabinet, along with the half-empty can of Gillette Foamy shaving cream.

He pushed the button on top of the can, and the heavy whipped foam sputtered into the hollow of his hand. He laid the foam on his beard like a refinisher lays on paint remover—thick, putting it down in one long stroke. He pulled on the metal chain and the light glared, but the eyes in the mirror were darker now, livelier, and the face looked younger smeared with white foam.

Joe positioned the razor at the right side of his jaw, just under his ear, and pulled the skin taut with one hand, while he drew the blade down across his jawline. The blade left a smooth, reddened trail through the white cream. He finished shaving his face and moved to his upper lip. He held his nose tip with one finger, pushing up, while he stiffened his lip and shaved in a series of short, downward strokes. He rinsed the razor, unscrewing the head, so the blade wouldn't rust, and put it back into the cabinet. He filled his cupped hands with cold water and splashed his face, then reached for a worn hand towel that hung on a cup hook by the mirror and rubbed his face dry. Joe opened the cabinet again, and took out a black, Ace pocket comb and ran it through his tousled hair, until it was tamed. Whistling, he went back into the main room and pulled on his jeans, carefully tucking the work shirttails into his waistband and zipping his fly with a satisfied yank. He was just pulling on his best cowboy boots, when Walters burst into the room.

Walters stopped in his tracks when he saw Joe.

"What happened to you, Rizzo?" Walters asked, staring slack-jawed, a wet cigar hanging dangerously from the corner of his mouth.

Joe grinned and went back to pulling on his right boot.

Walters pulled the cigar out of his mouth and threw it on the floor. It rolled soggily into the corner and smothered in a pile of dirt.

"Damn it all, Rizzo! I *knew* you'd been holdin' out on me! OK, who is she?"

"Who's who?" Joe asked, standing up and shaking his pant legs down over his boot tops.

"Cut it out, Joe. This is me, Walters; you can level with me. I bet it's that dame over in Woodward—what's-her-name—the babe with the figure that won't quit. That's who it is, isn't it, Rizzo?"

"Who what is?"

"The one who wrote the letter—"

"Letter?"

"Damn you, Rizzo! You *know* what letter!"

"Oh, *that* letter." Joe smiled, picked up his change, wallet, and car keys from the table top next to the stuffed chair. "I told you it was probably nothing, and it was. An advertising gimmick, just like I said. Trying to get me to buy some perfume called 'Spring Garden.' Had some kind of paper towel inside the envelope saturated with the stuff. I probably won't get the smell out of here for weeks."

Walters followed Rizzo out of the door, and to his truck—a 1968 Chevrolet pickup, red, with a dented hood, and rust stains on the doors, where the paint had been scratched. The rain had stopped, and over in the west, it looked like the sun was trying to shove a few rays through the clouds.

"OK, I'll buy that for now, . . . but, Rizzo, if that's all it was, why are you all decked out and headin' for—where are you headed for, Rizzo?"

"Woodward," Joe said, climbing in his truck and slamming the door.

"I knew it! I knew it was that babe in Woodward, you S.O.B! What's her name?"

"Shelly."

"Yeah, that's it . . . Shelly. Writes a hot letter, huh?" Walters's face twisted into a leer.

"Told you, Walters, the letter was a perfume ad, that's all. Shelly had nothing to do with it." Joe turned the key in the ignition and revved the engine.

"Then why?"

"Just felt like going out tonight, that's all. Can't a guy just want to get out of this dump without the third degree?"

"Sure, Rizzo, but—"

"But it's like you said, Walters: there comes a time when a man's got to consider certain things, sort of take stock. I'm not getting any younger, and I just decided I didn't want to spend all my time getting drunk and seeing nothing prettier than the likes of you . . . You really ought to be a philosopher, Walters. You have a way of making a man think." Rizzo flashed Walters a smile, put the pickup into reverse, and backed out of the motel parking slot. He shifted into first gear, then into second, and stepped down hard on the accelerator.

Five miles out of town, cruising at a good clip over the trafficless, two-lane blacktop toward Woodward, Joe reached inside his shirt pocket and pulled out the letter, carefully folded in half. He shook the envelope and the cardboard sandwich fell out on the seat. Joe reached over and pulled out the picture of his family. He looked at it in the growing dusk and put it back into his pocket. Then he took the letter and the envelope, wadded them into a pink ball with one large hand, rolled down the window, and tossed it out. Joe watched in the rearview mirror as the wind caught it, blowing it down the road like a tumbleweed, until it blew into a ditch, where he lost sight of it as he rounded the curve that led toward Woodward.

The End